Bound & Gagged

Jamila Jasper

Copyright © 2017 Jamila Jasper Romance

All rights reserved.

ISBN: 9781521725498

This paperback was updated February 6th 2018.

Dedicated to my mailing list subscribers, especially Gail, Andrea, Donna, T, Anna and the loyal team of advanced reviewers.

You can find Jamila Jasper online:

Website: Www.jamilajasperromance.com

Twitter: www.twitter.com/jamilajasper

YouTube: http://bit.ly/2CdKJUM

Instagram: www.instagram.com/BWWMJamila

Facebook: https://www.facebook.com/BWWMJamila/

Patreon: www.patreon.com/jamilajasper

Pinterest: www.pinterest.com/jamilajasper

Prologue: Benjamin's Beginnings

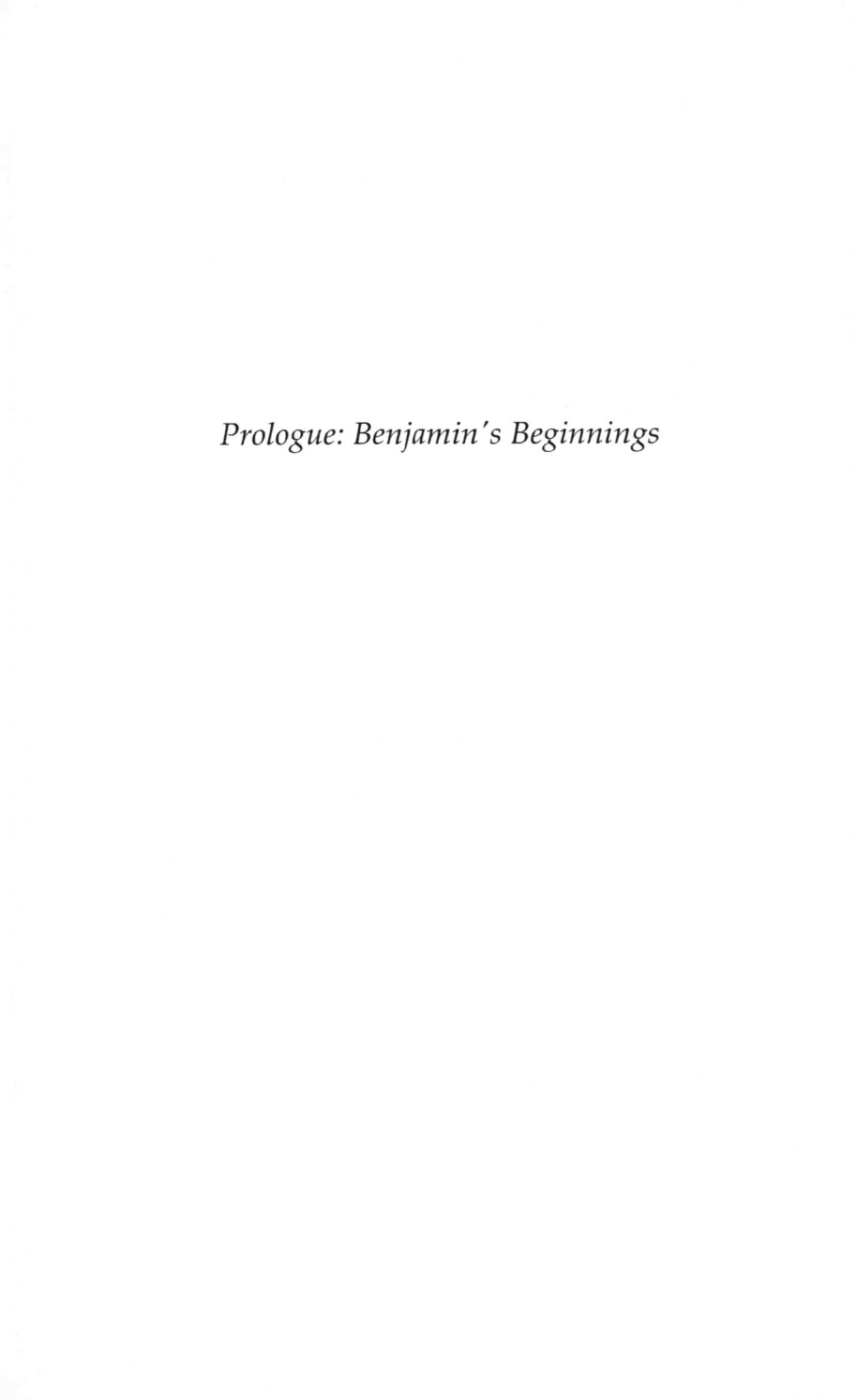

The day I closed the restaurant deal was the best day of my life. I felt like I'd scammed my way into a group of elites, sitting at that table with some of the biggest investors in the game. My father had helped me get a meeting with these guys — some of the top shots in the industry. Craig Gordon, Timothy Patton and Kyle Lyman grilled me for hours, quizzed me on the minutia of my business plan until they were satisfied that I really had my shit together.

And then they signed. And I signed. And then I had the green light to open three new restaurants. The one in Dallas was going right between a shitty Thai takeout spot and a barbershop. The one in Las Vegas was on an upscale street, in a spot my guys had picked out just for the restaurant. The third place was a wild card restaurant in Oklahoma City where I'd be opening the only French restaurant for twenty miles. It was safe to say these openings would be a huge success and the investor's were over the moon about me.

What can I say, I'm a charismatic guy. I could charm the hooves off a horse with my eyes closed and my tongue cut out.

When I started my French restaurants at twenty, I had no idea how big they'd get. In our city, the restaurant business is tough. And I knew that. My dad gave me $200,000 to get started and I paid the loan back within the first two years of business — with plenty of money left over for me to live the lifestyle that I wanted.

Now that I was franchising the business, I knew I'd have even more rest and relaxation ahead. I was well on my way to my goal of retiring at forty. Now I could finally spend some time settling down, maybe even find the right girl. The right girl wasn't easy to find. I've been dating Kim for the past three years and she's a nice enough girl but there's something about her that's very vanilla.

She's exactly the type of girl you'd expect me to date. I know where I stand, and I'm a perfect ten. I'm 6'5", I've got millions in the bank from my business and I drive a brand new BMW that I trade in every three years. I'm a catch, especially in this city where most men can hardly hold down a job and even if they can, half their paychecks go straight to their student loans. Bullshit. I might not have a college degree, but I get how to live a good life. And a good life is lived hard and fast.

* * *

So right, I was telling you about Kim. Kim's alright. She's 5'4", she's got mousy brown hair and plain pale skin with freckles all over it. She's got a nice body — maybe too nice — and she works at one of the private universities coaching water polo in the winter and tennis in the spring. As I said, Kim is vanilla. But she's hot. Vanilla in bed, but hot. She's exactly the kind of girl the big shots expect me to have on my arm so I keep her around even if she's convinced that I treat her like shit.

But Kim knows the deal. She's my girl, my main girl, but of course I have other chicks in rotation. What can she expect? Her job is so demanding that she can't cater to my every need. Other women keep me sane. Aside from Kim, I've been dating Camilla, Joan and Megan.

Or maybe it's spelled Meghan with an "h". Hell if I remember. I barely see Megan (or Meghan) anyways.

Camilla is Puerto Rican with this sweet buttery smooth accent. I like when we're doing it and she whimpers in that soft breathy voice calling me "papi" over and over again. Joan is a solid 4/10, but she's good in bed and likes all the kinky stuff that I like. I can't keep her around for too long 'cause she gets clingy. I'm too much of a free spirit for that. And Megan? (Or is it Meghan?) She's a girl I picked up from the rougher side of town. She's skinny, dark-skinned, and loves lavish dates and even more lavish nights. She's expensive, but at least she's given me a chance to diversify the kind of girls I get into, if you know what I mean.

* * *

As I drove back to my condo, I scrolled through the numbers in my phone. I needed to choose the right girl for the night and I wasn't sure if Kim would do.

Kim was great, but I didn't want her to mistake this for me settling down. I liked all the girls in my life well enough but I had no plans to settle down with any of them. Especially not Kim.

But I called her. What else could she be doing on a night like this. When she picked up, I chuckled at the frustration in her voice.

"What is it Benji?"

(She insisted upon calling me that stupid nickname. Something she picked up from my mom who insisted that I marry her before she got too old.)

"Come over," I demanded.

Asking nicely never got anything done. With women, you had to show them that you knew exactly what you wanted and you were willing to do anything to get it.

Kim sighed. I could tell she was playing up her resistance for the sake of it.
"Why should I come over Benji?" She whined. And she used that nickname again. She was starting to get on my nerves.

"If you don't want to come over I'll call someone else."

I moved to hang up, but Kim wasn't going to

knowingly see another one of my girls on her watch.

"Wait!" She stopped me, "I'll come over. Fine."

"Twenty minutes."

"Benji, I need time to get ready," She whined again.

"Twenty minutes," I repeated. This wasn't up for debate or discussion. I had good news to share and I wanted a beautiful woman to share it with.

I hung up on her then before she got a chance to protest. Kim knew what she was getting being with me, and I hated when she pretended that she didn't.

* * *

I arrived at the condo, pulled into the garage and walked upstairs. I clapped, turning on the lights. I couldn't wait for an upgrade. Two years into the restaurant franchising, I envisioned a big upgrade. I already had an architect friend of mine drawing up the plans for my palazzo.

I took a quick, ice-cold shower and changed into a white oxford and khakis. I ignored calls from my father and from my brother, turning instead towards my wine rack. I wanted to select something with body for our evening together.

On my security cameras, I saw Kim pull up with her five-year old Toyota Corolla that I'd given her a grand to fix last month. She looked piss, even in the grainy image on the camera. As she waltzed up to my front door with visible frustration, I wracked my brain for what petty drama she'd managed to concoct about our relationship. Kim was always doing shit like that. We saw our situation differently, that was it.

"Open the door Benji!" She screeched, after I watched her a few moments on the camera.

She knew I was watching her.

I pushed the button on my security system and the door swung open. Kim took her shoes off and came right to the kitchen. Just as I predicted, she was in a *mood.* And it was one of those moods. I wondered if she was menstruating but thought it would be bad form to check my calendar for her right in front of her.

* * *

"Good evening princess," I said with a grin.

She refused to return the smile.

"You. Are. An. ASSHOLE!" She screeched.

I tried to hold back a smirk. The last time I'd pissed Kim off, she'd hit me with her purse until I apologized. I'd learned my lesson.

"What's wrong?"

"Threatening me with other girls just so I come over?"

"Honesty is the cornerstone of our arrangement," I replied.

* * *

Kim's face turned beet-red.

"Arrangement?!" Kim screamed, "This isn't an arrangement Benji. This is a *relationship.*"

See? I told you we saw things differently.

"Uhh," I tried to buy myself time.

"Jesus Benji! You're always doing this to me! You have me sitting here like we're going to get *married!*" She continued yelling at me. I didn't know if I'd ever get her to quiet down.

"I wanted to tell you something today," I said quietly.

I saw a tiny glimmer of hope in Kim's eyes. She stopped yelling at me and folded her arms. I wasn't out of the woods yet.

"What is it you wanted to tell me?" She asked.

I sighed.

"I closed the deal. We're franchising. Three new restaurants across the United States."

"Really?" Kim asked.

"Yes, really."

"Benji! Oh my goodness!" She squealed.

She leaped towards me and wrapped her arms around me. I still had my doubts that this would last long. She held me in her arms and I reached down to kiss her forehead. I don't know how I managed to stay so detached from Kim when it was clear she was more than attached to me.

She pulled away and I even saw tears in her eyes (poor thing).

"That's amazing Benji… I'm so proud of you."

"You always believed in me."

And then my phone rang. Shit. It was Megan. Her number flashed across the screen, along with her name.

Kim's eyes darted to the phone and whatever good will I'd built up with her was torn down in an instant. Shit.

"Megan?" She asked, "Who's Megan?"

* * *

I snatched my phone off the counter.

"Don't worry about it. Tonight is about celebrating."

"I ASKED YOU WHO THE HELL IS MEGAN!" Kim screamed again.

Her face was red all over again. Her voice reverberated through my condo and I knew I was in for a long night.

"She's just a friend," I replied.

I tried to feel guilty as I said the words. I tried to feel guilty as I remembered Megan stripping down to nothing before me and allowing me to tie her up with thick black ropes.

* * *

"She's just a friend?" Kim asked — there was that hopeful tone of voice again.

"Yeah. Just a friend."

"You're a lying bastard!" She screamed back at me.

"Kim! Can you please calm down!"

"NO!" She yelled, "Don't tell me to calm down! I know you're lying to me. I know you're sleeping with her! I know that you're probably sleeping with half the bitches in this city!"

"Kim!"

I knew I wouldn't get through to her. But Kim

was like this. She'd cry. And then I'd start kissing her. Then, she'd forget all of it. She knew I didn't love her. She knew that we weren't going to spend the rest of our lives together. She knew all of this. But she still came. She still came into my life and into my bed over and over again. She loved this game — as did I.

Maybe one day I'd settle down, but it wouldn't be tonight.

Kim continued yelling at me, "Fuck you! Fuck you! Fuck you!"

"KIM!"

"NO! Don't you dare call my name Benji! I've done everything for you. I've done everything…"

She started to break down. Tears filled her soft round eyes and I tried to take a step closer to her to calm her down.

"STAY AWAY FROM ME BENJI."

"What?"

"You're sick! You're sick!"

"Can you please calm the hell down?"

She started crying softer now, and she stopped yelling. I breathed a sigh of relief. The last thing I wanted to deal with was Kim's hysteria while I was supposed to be celebrating.

* * *

"Do you think you'll ever do it Benji?" She asked through her tears.

"Do what?" I replied.

"Settle down. Get married?"

I bit down on my lower lip. I hated when Kim asked questions like this and she knew it. I preferred to live in the moment. I preferred to live in a world where it didn't matter what I did in the future. I wanted fun, hot sex, hot women and a metric fuck-ton of money.

"No. I don't think so," I replied.

The honesty hurt me more than it hurt her. I just didn't show it.

* * *

She let out a piercing scream. This time, I didn't try to calm her down.

"You're broken," She replied through her tears.

I couldn't lie to her and tell her she was wrong.

"You do everything for mommy and daddy's love because you're just some fucked up rich kid. I actually love you Benji… I *loved* you. I thought that somehow I could change you. But you just want to be a fucked up player. You just want to break hearts."

"That's not true," I said weakly, unsure of whether or not she was right.

Kim looked at me with anger in her eyes that I'd never seen before, "Don't bullshit me Benji. I know you. And I know you're such a piece of *shit* that you'll never settle down. It would take a real crazy bitch to figure out what the fuck makes you tick."

"Kim…"

"Shut up! I'm done with you Benjamin. I'm done. This is it."

"So you're leaving?"

Kim picked up her purse and nodded, "Yes. I'm leaving."

I sighed and she saw my relief wash over my face. That hurt her more than me being an asshole.
"I hope you find someone."

I wanted to wish her the same, but I couldn't.

She repeated, "I hope you find someone that can change that fucked up little head of yours. Not every woman will be like your mother Benjamin. Give someone a chance before you die alone like every other rich asshole."

And then she turned around and left. I wanted to stop her, but I couldn't. Maybe I just knew that I'd put Kim through enough. She'd been through hell and back because of me, and I knew I'd reached the point in time when I needed to stop hurting her. She'd snapped — finally. I couldn't bear to pick up my phone or to call any of my other girls. I knew I deserved her wrath.

* * *

And maybe, for the first time, Kim had gotten through to me just like she'd always hoped she would. Was I really destined to die alone? Was I really going to waste my youth chasing after shallow women and cheap sex? Was that really it? Kim had a point. A good point. But that didn't mean I wanted her to be my one and only. Just as I'd told her, that was never going to be a part of my plan.

When she left, I walked to the front door and watched her car zoom away. I stepped out of the front door and breathed in the fresh air. I looked in my mailbox and saw an envelope that I'd left there for the past three days. I knew what it was, but I'd refused to pick it up. Today was the day.

I picked up the envelope and returned inside with my celebratory bottle of wine which I'd now be drinking alone. I didn't bother pouring a glass. I sat at the barstool in my kitchen and drank straight from the bottle. I got about halfway through before opening the envelope.

You are cordially invited to the wedding of Mr. Y. Hawthorne & Ms. K. Shepherd
June 1st, 2018

I stopped reading before I hit the address and I ignored the "RSVP" date. My brother would know that I was coming. Heck, I'm sure he'd prefer if I *didn't* RSVP.

I couldn't believe the bastard was getting married already. The worst part was not being able to understand why. I lived a hell of a life as a bachelor. Why wouldn't my brother Yates want a part of this?

* * *

I finished the bottle of wine alone and passed out on the couch.

1 Crashing Down

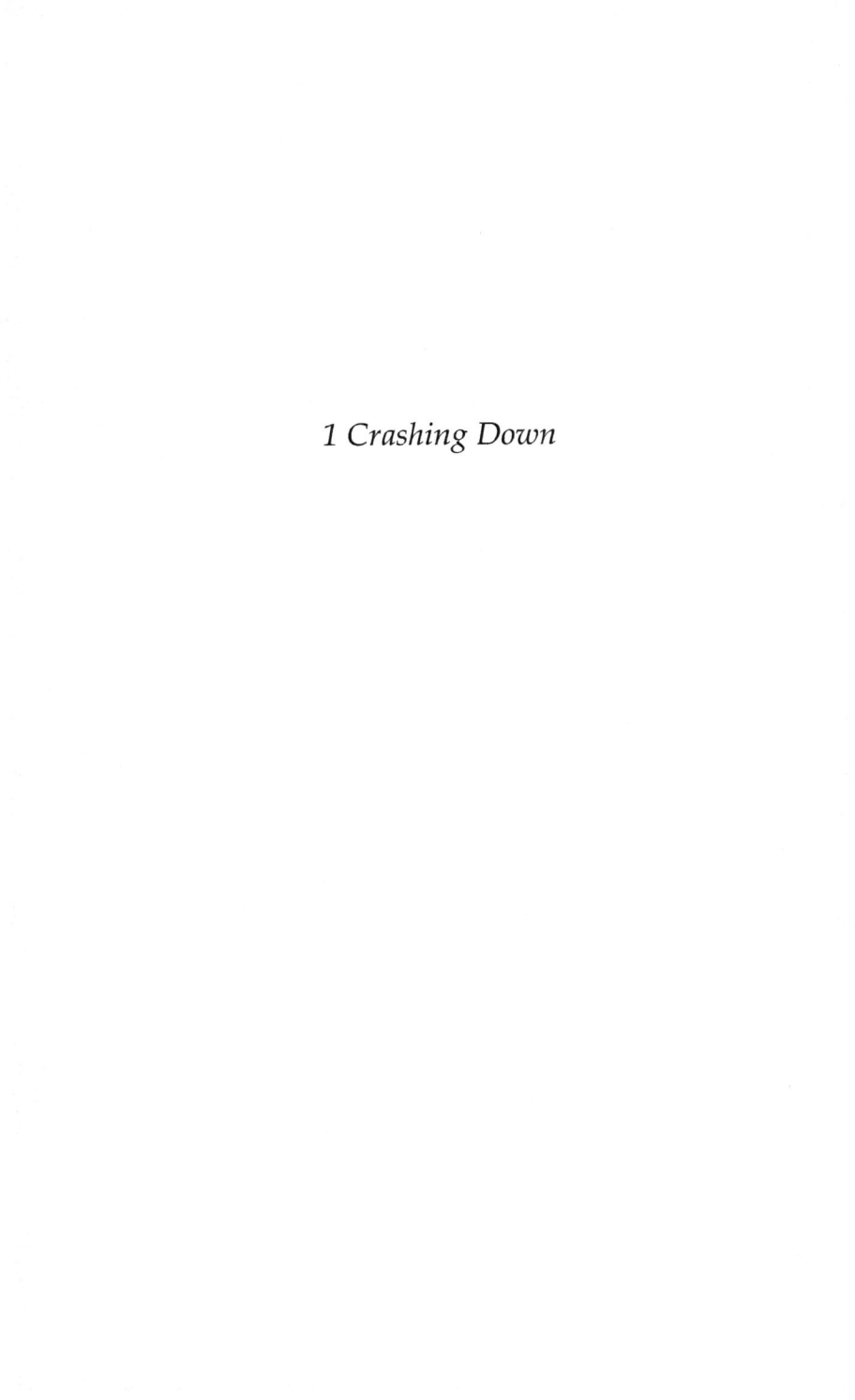

Hawthorne's was a French restaurant on the other side of town that had been around for 3 years. May Roberts had never been to Hawthorne's but it was the restaurant that men took women to that they wanted to impress. May wondered why her date hadn't put effort into other things to impress her.

She was sitting across from him, at the table he'd reserved in the most crowded part of the restaurant. He'd been rude to the hostess from the time that they'd walked into the place, creating an uncomfortable vibe instantly.

May knew she should have ignored Kristin's advice completely when it came to dating. Kristin was getting married to your classic exceedingly wealthy white guy. Now that May's best friend was getting married, she felt like the pressure was on to find a guy to settle down with. When Kristin had suggested May go out with Khalil, May had been convinced that it was only because they were both black. Khalil was nice and all, but May didn't think they'd have anything in common.

Forty-five minutes into their date, May was starting to see that she was right. Kristin's well intentioned attempt at setting up a date was starting to look like an abject failure.

"It's a shame black queens these days are all turning into bed wenches…"

May was shaken out of her distracted daydream by Khalil's conversation starter.

"Huh?" She replied.

* * *

"Bed wenches. All these females want to do is find some white man to play slave with."

May's eyes widened. Was someone actually saying something so ignorant in this day and age. Thinking that there was a chance she misunderstood, she asked Khalil to clarify.

"What are you talking about? Are you saying that all women in interracial relationships are bed wenches?"

May felt dirty just repeating the phrase out loud.

Khalil shrugged, "Don't worry. This isn't about you. You're not that kind of woman… I can tell. Look at you on a date with a handsome, strong black king."

"Right."

May downed half her wine glass. She didn't think she'd be able to make it through this meal without two more of these.

Khalil went on for a few more minutes until finally, their entrees had arrived. May tried not to say much as she ate, but that didn't stop Khalil from spilling his philosophical tirades throughout the meal. May was looking for an escape route…fast.

When Khalil started off a sentence with "Jews control everything…", May thought it might be a good time to excuse herself to the bathroom. Khalil seemed content to let her go and unsuspecting that she was really heading there to work out her escape plan.

Once in the rest room, May let out a loud sigh. Agreeing to this date was a bad idea. Khalil had looked good on paper, but that should have been a clear red flag. Guys who looked good on paper rarely ever measured up in real life. And now, she'd resigned herself to an evening of conspiracy theories and bizarre old school prejudices.

May couldn't believe that she'd actually dressed up for this date. She looked in the mirror at the new dress she'd picked out. The forest green color complemented the rich, cool undertones of her dark skin perfectly. The dress hugged her figure without showing off everything and she'd felt more confident than she had in months. Too bad that confidence was being wasted on a guy who felt like interracial relationships were the scourge of the earth.

May pulled out her phone and called Kristin. After a few rings Kristin picked up.

"Hey girl, how's the date?"

"It's awful!" May hissed, "Do you know what this guy is like?!"

"He's sooo nice!" Kristin cooed.

May rolled her eyes and tried to get Kristin to focus, "He isn't nice at all Kristin! He's insane. I promise."

"Are you sure you're not just raising your standards too high?!"

"I'm sure," May assured her, "Please can we just go through our emergency bad-date procedure?"

Kristin sighed, "Sure. I really thought you guys would hit it off."

"Thanks."

May hung up. She wasn't about to lecture Kristin on her soft-racism just yet. Kristin had her air-headed moments of thinking that May would get along with any guy just because he was black, but overall she was a well-meaning small town white girl who had been a loyal friend to May since college. (It was hard to imagine how long ago these days were.)

* * *

May fixed her hair a bit and then washed her hands before returning to her date. Khalil was waiting for her eagerly with a smile on his face that was unmistakably lust-filled. May sighed and sat down.

"I was waiting for you to get back," Khalil said, cracking her a smile and then reaching his hand over to touch May's thighs.

She jerked her leg away. She had just met Khalil and the last thing she wanted was his hand anywhere near her thighs.

"Great."

May couldn't figure out what she was doing that was turning Khalil on, but she wanted to stop doing it as soon as possible. She powered through the rest of her entree, trying to ignore Khalil's rant about how the earth was really flat, and that round earth was a white male conspiracy. May was getting tired of his delusions of persecution, and desperate for Kristin to stop playing matchmaker and pull the trigger on her escape plan.

"So," Khalil started, clearing his throat, "May I ask why a beautiful black queen such as yourself is wearing a weave?"

May looked up at Khalil with a raised eyebrow. His personality was such a shame. Khalil was actually a good looking guy, he had a good job and he drove a nice car. Unfortunately, his attitude stank, and May was just about getting sick of it.

Right before she could tell Khalil off for

thinking he could come to her about her hair choices, her phone rang. It was Kristin.

"Hold on, I need to take this," May said.

She picked up the phone and feigned concern, "Hello? Hello is everything okay?"

She stood up and gestured to Khalil that she would be heading outside to take the phone call. Khalil nodded.

May took a few steps away from him, barely paying attention as she weaved through the tables in the restaurant.

"Girl it took you long enough…"

"Did it work?"

***

"I'm walking away from the table right now… We need to think of an excuse."

"Uhh," Kristin tried to be helpful, "My cat died. And uh…. you need to help me through the grief!"

"Let's hope that works…" May mumbled.

"I just don't get what you don't like about him!"

Before May could explain, her lack of attention to where she was going caught up with her. Her heel caught on the tablecloth of the table she was walking past and before she knew it, her legs had flown out from under her and she landed face first on the ground.

***

"May? May?" She could hear Kristin's voice from her phone which had flown a few feet away from her on the floor.

Following her thud to the ground, the entire table she slipped by came crashing down. Crystal wine glasses, fine china and candles fell to the floor and all shattered around her. Everyone in the restaurant turned from their tables and all eyes were focused on May.

She tried to get up, but only stumbled again.

"Ow!" She cried out.

The man whose table she'd upset crouched down as various waiters and waitresses bustled around cleaning up the mess.

* * *

"Are you alright!?" He asked.

May looked up into the man's eyes.

"Yes… I'm okay… I think…"

"Here, let me help you."

"Thanks," May mumbled, "Gosh this is so embarrassing."

As if the situation couldn't have grown any worse, as the man helped May to her feet, Khalil came rushing over from his side of the restaurant.

"Hey man, get your hands off her," He said to the man who was actually helping May off the ground.

* * *

The man kept his hands on May, unmoved by Khalil's threatening posture.

"Are you alright?" Khalil asked, taking May's hands into his own.

"Yeah," May mumbled, "But my leg hurts. Could you grab my phone for me?"

The man who had helped May up took a step back and Khalil went to grab her phone. May tried to dust off her dress and ignore the stares of the people whose eyes were still glued to the scene. Khalil handed May back her cellphone.

"Thanks."

"Queen, shall we return to the table?"
May saw her opportunity to get out of this date.

Finally.

She faked a wince and crumpled to the ground again. The man whose table she'd upset rushed to her side.

"You know what buddy," He said, "It looks like she's in a lot of pain. Why don't you square off the bill and we'll make sure she gets home."

Khalil tried to argue with the guy, but he just didn't have it in him. Waves of relief overcame May to the point where she didn't bother trying to argue on Khalil's behalf.

"Maybe we'll do it again some time…" She offered weakly.

Defeated, Khalil walked back to their table to

take his jacket and to pay off the rest of their bill.

"Bad date?" The man who had helped said.

"Huh?" May replied.

"Sorry," The man said, "My name is Benjamin. You can call me Ben."

"May. Nice to meet you. And I'm so so sorry for ruining dinner."

Ben seemed to be amused at the idea that she'd ruined his dinner.

"You didn't ruin anything. But you also didn't answer my question. Bad date?"

May nodded, "Yeah."

"Don't worry, we'll make sure he's gone before we get you home. Sit at my table."

Ben pulled out a chair for May to sit on and then helped her into it. May had a notion that he knew she was faking how badly her leg hurt, but he didn't seem to care. Ben walked over to Khalil who was near the register. May looked over at him as he spoke to Khalil, shook the man's hand and then eventually, took out his own credit card to pay.

Khalil walked out of the restaurant, barely looking back at May. Once he was gone, May again felt relief wash over her. The date was over. Her public humiliation at least had one benefit.

* * *

By the time Ben returned to the table, the waitstaff had cleaned up the mess completely and set his table with a fresh set of dressings.

"Well, I got rid of your date," Ben replied with a smile.

"Thanks. How did you know that guy wasn't my boyfriend or something?"

Ben chuckled, "Well if he was your boyfriend, you didn't like him very much considering the lengths you went to in order to get away from him."

May lowered her head bashfully, "I didn't cause a scene on purpose."

* * *

"I know," Ben said, "But you were clearly miserable. I've been watching you from the time you got in here."

"Oh…"

Ben didn't seem phased by May's uncertainty.

"I can tell when a woman is into a man and when she isn't. That guy… he's not for you."

"Not for me? What do you mean?"

"I can tell what a woman like you wants and it isn't the kind of guy who will make you cause a scene just to get away from him."

"Maybe you have a point."

* * *

"Is your leg really okay?"

"Yeah, I think so. But I may have broken my heel."

May bent over to take a closer look at her shoes. Sure enough, the heel that had caught on the table cloth had snapped off from the sole of her shoe. Great, like this wasn't embarrassing enough, she'd have to find her way home with only one shoe.

"Why don't I take you home then," Ben replied.

"Oh…" May muttered awkwardly.

She liked Ben well enough but she'd just met the guy. She didn't want to get in his car, much less show him where her house was. This is how women ended up on the evening news and that wasn't the way that May wanted to go out.

"Listen, I'm betting you're thinking that you have no reason to trust me, and I could be a crazy ax-murderer just priming you for a midnight feast."

"Um…" May tried to buy time, not wanting to admit that was exactly what she'd been thinking.

"I get it. But you still need a way to get home because if you had a way home by now you would have told me to take a hike."

"Right…"

"Well live a little. Listen, I'm not the kind of guy you think I am. I'll just take you home and… that will be it."

"If I get into your car, how can I be sure you won't kill me?"

Ben grinned. He could tell that May was uncomfortable, but attracted to him. He saw the way she looked away from him when she spoke, how her fingers couldn't stop twirling around her hair and how she bit down on her lower lip every time he opened his mouth to say something. That was alright. He liked that she was attracted to him. But he didn't like this little mind game she was playing. It was clear that he wasn't a dusty criminal. He was a well to-do guy offering to drop her off. Sure, Ben wanted more, but he knew that May hadn't yet figured that out.

* * *

"Listen. You can take a picture of my license plate and send it to the girl friend who almost bailed you out of here."

May was going to ask how Ben knew she was on the phone with a girl friend, but he had already demonstrated that his powers of observation were keen. If not keen, then freakish.

"Right. Well I guess for now I'll trust you."

Ben smiled and stood up, offering May a hand. She took his hand and stood up.

"Can you stand on that foot?"

"I might need a little help."

* * *

Ben was more than happy to support May on the way out of the restaurant. May noticed that Ben had left without paying, but none of the waitresses stopped him. *Strange.* May leaned on Ben and felt the strength of his muscles as she held onto him. She'd been ignoring it for a while, but now, May was forced to admit to herself that Ben was *sexy*. He wasn't just casually good looking, he was *stunning*. He was the kind of guy that would make men and women alike lick their lips with arousal when they saw him.

May walked out to the parking lot and she looked around to see if she could guess which car Ben was driving. He seemed well off. And there was something *different* about him, but she lacked his observational skills to figure out exactly what that was.

* * *

Ben reached into his pocket and clicked the button to unlock his car. Lights flared up, and May couldn't avoid noticing which car he was leading to. The posh, white BMW looked brand new. May's eyes widened.

Ben walked to the car and then gestured, "Hold on."

He stood next to the bumper.

"Come on, take your picture. Make sure you're going home with a guy who isn't a maniac."

May reached into her pocket for her phone. She took a picture of Ben and the car's license plate but she didn't send it to Kristin. She didn't want Kristin to know that she'd taken a *massive* detour from Khalil. Instead, May sent the picture to one of her other friends, Martha. At least Martha wouldn't judge her for taking such a massive 180 degree turn from her originally planned date.

"Great. Sent the picture."

"Excellent. Let me get your door and I'll help you get over there."

Ben walked over to her door and then pulled it open. May was starting to sense that Ben was attracted to her. There was no need for him to be doing all of this, but he was acquiescing with a smile on his face.

Hopefully there really is nothing wrong with him. May thought to herself.

* * *

She leaned on Ben as he walked her to the car and helped her into the plush leather front seat.

"Ahh…"

"Take your shoes off. Kick back. Make yourself comfortable."

Wouldn't she? The interior of Ben's car was exquisite. As May leaned back into the seat, she felt like she'd entered another planet of luxury. She took her shoes off and p spread her toes out, curling them up after. May let out a loud sigh of relief. She was no longer on a date with Khalil, and more exciting, she was in the car with an *incredibly* good looking guy.

Ben got into the driver's seat and May got a

proper look at him again. Ben was at least 6'5", she had gathered that from leaning on him. His body was pure lean muscle. There was not an ounce of fat on him; May could tell from his well-fitted designer clothing. He had well kept brown hair that was cropped short and brilliant olive green eyes, alive with energy and infused with amber flecks in the sunlight.

Ben turned to look at her and smiled, "So, where exactly are we bringing Frostbite here."

"Frostbite?"

"What kind of decent guy doesn't give his car a name?" Ben replied with a wink.

"Right," May said, "Uhh… Let me type in my address."

* * *

She reached forward and plugged her address into Ben's GPS, fully aware of the size of the risk she was taking. Ben started to drive, and turned to look at May. He could sense May's attraction to him and he wanted to turn the conversation in that direction quickly before he ran out of time. She was gorgeous.

May had a gorgeous body with a slim waist and a nice round butt. Her eyes were soft and gentle and her cheeks were round too. Ben also loved May's gorgeous dark skin which was a sun kissed umber color that highlighted her deep features. She was put together for her date — nothing too revealing. Ben loved the way her forest green dress hugged her curves but he could stand to see her in something else… something a bit sexier.

* * *

"So… You walked out of that place without paying," May started.

She wasn't sure if it was an awkward question to ask, but she couldn't help herself. She had never met anyone as cavalier and suave as Ben.

"Yes, I did. Very observant," He replied cheekily.

May tried asking again, "Why? Are you some kind of restaurant kleptomaniac."

"No."

"You're teasing me," May said, chuckling.

Ben chuckled back, "Fine. You caught me. I'm

a tease. I own the place."

"You *own* Hawthorne's?!"

"What? You sound surprised."

"I guess I pictured a small old Frenchman…"

Ben laughed, "Sorry to disappoint. No, my mother's French. My dad's American. I started Hawthorne's when I was twenty and never looked back."

"Wow. It's a lovely restaurant."

"Thank you," Ben said, "But I don't want to talk about my restaurant. I want to talk about you."

"Me?"

"Sure. I want to get to know you."

"Is that why you agreed to drive me home?"

Ben nodded, "Yup. This was all a cheap ploy."

May felt heat rising to her cheeks, "Wow. At least you're honest."

"Damn right I am," Ben said, "So tell me about yourself… May."

"May Roberts. And uh… I'm a financial analyst for a big company in the city."

"Wow," Ben said, "Sounds like hard work."

"It is hard work. But it's rewarding."

* * *

"But if you could… would you quit? If you had all the money in the world?"

May found the question a bit odd, and quite personal, but she couldn't help but answer Ben's question. Something about him was beyond compelling — he was magnetizing in every way.

"Yes, of course I could. Wouldn't everyone say that?"

Ben laughed, "Not me. I love my business. It's like cocaine to me."

"Wow."

Ben noticed that May was falling silent. That

wouldn't do. The more he heard her honey-sweet voice and the more he watched the evening sun dance across her umber skin, the more he wanted to warm her up so he could spend the night with her. She was gorgeous. And he'd never wanted any woman as much as he wanted May. This time, it was more than the chase for Ben. He felt a deep internal compulsion to pursue her with all his might.

"Listen May," Ben continued, "What on earth were you doing on a date with a guy like Khalil?"

"Really? We have to talk about this?"

"Hell yeah we do," Ben replied.

May let out a loud sigh.

*　*　*

"He's just someone my friend set me up with. She thinks that I've been single too long."

"Have you?"

May looked at him, unsure if she was really ready to disclose all her personal business to a man she'd just met.

"Dunno. I've been single for three years… But I've been happy. You don't know how relieving it is not to have to deal with assholes who are only there for a quick screw and never call you back."

Ben changed the subject fast.

"Like jazz?"

* * *

"Hm?" May replied.

She was still distracted, thinking about her three-year period of solitude. Ben pushed a few buttons on his screen and the car was filled with the sonorous piano, and then Billie Holiday's voice.

"I *love* Billie Holiday," May said.

She closed her eyes and hummed the melody of the song.

Summertime… when the living is easy…

"So you do like jazz?" Ben asked.

May nodded, "Oh yes. I've got an old vinyl

collection that would probably scare you."

May collected vinyl records like some women collected shoes. With her very first paycheck, she'd purchased a Prince record on vinyl and since then, her love of vinyl had been cemented.

Ben shifted in his seat and looked over at May with renewed lust.

"So… Who else do you like besides Billie Holiday?"

"Are you testing me?"

"Maybe," Ben smirked.

"Theophilus Monk, Etta James, Bessie Smith…"

"You listen to Bessie Smith? Old school blues?"

May chuckled, "Yes, why wouldn't I?"

"Dunno,' Ben said and shrugged.

May reached for the knobs on the radio and turned the music up. They drove for two or three more songs. Traffic was heavier than usual, but it gave May enough time to think about what was happening here. Maybe it was the music, or maybe it was just something about Ben, but she was starting to feel a magnetic pulsing in her chest.

She was starting to feel like she *wanted* him. They hadn't been on a date together but from the time she'd met Ben there was something alluring about him. He took control of the whole situation with Khalil and before she could protest, he had been a white knight to her aid.

"We're almost there," Ben said to her with a smile.

"Right."

May stared at Ben's face, taking in the contours of his sharp jawline and cheekbones. She wanted him to come upstairs with her. She didn't *have* to sleep with him — just talk. Hey, he liked jazz after all. If a guy could fall in love with Billie Holiday's voice like she had, there had to be something right about him.

"How big is your vinyl collection?" Ben asked.

* * *

May snapped out of her head again.

"Big. Very big."

"I need to see it. I'm coming upstairs with you."

Whoa. That wasn't how May had expected things to happen. Ben had just invited himself upstairs before she'd figured out if she really wanted him in her apartment.

"Uhh… Are you sure? I have to go to work early tomorrow."

"Why?" Ben asked.

May was taken aback by his forward approach.

"Uh… I don't know!" May stumbled over her

words, "I just have to."

"You'll have to think of a better excuse next time," Ben said.

They pulled up in front of May's home. Ben seemed to be eyeing her house, perhaps looking for cues about her, or just out of curiosity.

"Big for one person," Ben said as he got out of the car and moved around to the other side. May didn't know how to respond to that. Her parents had helped her pay for the house but she didn't think it was particularly big for one person.

"I guess so," She replied to no one in particular.

Ben opened her car door and then helped her out.

* * *

"Not far to hobble," He said.

May smiled and then prepared to lean on his formidable frame once again. It felt good to have a man so close to her, especially after all this time out of the dating game. Ben was no ordinary guy either. He was more attractive than anyone May had ever been with. She had to admit to herself, after Khalil, pretty much any guy would have seemed like a relief.

Thank goodness, a man who isn't insane!

That was how May felt with Ben. But there was something else to. He loved jazz. He would go out of his way to help a woman in need just because. He could read her like a book.

* * *

Ben carried her to the front door and then asked, "Keys?"

"I'll get them from my purse."

May fumbled in her purse, watching her hands tremble gently as she reached for her key. She couldn't figure out why she felt so nervous. Ben was just coming in to take a look at her vinyl collection. That was it — maybe they'd pop a few records on — but there wouldn't be anything more to that.

May banished the intrusive thoughts that were telling her a kiss wouldn't hurt.

"Nice place," Ben asserted once he entered May's house.

* * *

He stood in her foyer with his hands in his pockets, taking in every inch of her wall space and home. The place was spotless, as usual, with New England country design. May flicked on the light and kept her eyes on Ben. If he was going to expose himself as a creepy killer, he'd probably start now.

"Wow," He said, "Well… Take me to the Etta James."

"Whiskey?"

"Bourbon. No ice," He replied.

May took her shoes off and walked into the living room. She gestured towards her eggshell colored sofa and offered Ben a seat.

* * *

"Thanks, but I think I'll take my station at the record player."

May's vinyl collection was the focal point of the room. Her shelves were organized by decade and then alphabetically by artist. Her record player was wiped clean and inside, there was *Purple Rain* — an artifact from last week's "date night" when May had danced alone in her undies to Prince for three hours.

Ben ran his hands through her records, searching for one that caught his eye, so May took that opportunity to pour them both glasses of bourbon. She hadn't quite reached Ben's level of appreciation for whiskey, so she added a bit of ginger ale to hers and copious amounts of ice. May always thought of her grandfather when she poured a glass of bourbon.

* * *

She re-emerged and found Ben placing a Whitney Houston record on her turntable.

"Modern," May said, "Bourbon?"

Ben walked towards her and grabbed the bourbon. Standing inches away from her, he was growing tired of playing this game. He wanted to take her now — sweep her off her feet and get those feet behind her head. Whitney Houston and bourbon was putting him in a mood that he no longer wanted to ignore.

Ben downed the glass in one big gulp and slammed it down on the shelf.

"Ah. Perfection."

* * *

"Aren't you supposed to sip bourbon?" May teased shyly.

Ben shook his head, "Sipping takes too long. I prefer to get my liquor hard… and fast…"

He moved closer to May and then plucked her drink from her hand, setting it down next to his empty glass.

"Ben…" She started.

"Don't say anything," He replied, "Just let this happen… And admit you always knew this was going to happen."

May closed her eyes and allowed Ben's lips to touch hers. Holy shit. Kissing him send jolts of electric energy surging through her body, forcing her to stand at attention. May pulled away with widened eyes. For something so wrong, it felt so right.

"Ben, we can't do this. We just met," May whispered.

"Then why does it feel like we've known each other a thousand years?"

This time, he grabbed her. Ben clutched May's waist as he pulled her close to him and kissed her. This time, his tongue thrust down her throat and her heart ached with anxiety and excitement. He was right — she didn't want to say no.

May pressed her palms against Ben's chest. She felt his lion's heart beating slow and dull. He was calm, as if he'd orchestrated the entire evening. He felt none of her prey animal jitters, just desire.

"Please… We need to stop."

"Why…" He growled, his lips pressed to May's neck as he sucked her flesh between them.

"Ohhh," May moaned, as his tongue flicked over one of the most sensitive spots on her neck.

She didn't recall what question he'd asked. Ben's hands clutched her ass cheeks and he lifted her off the ground. May wrapped her thighs tightly around his muscled physique and allowed him to kiss her like this. Ben pressed her against the nearest wall and allowed his fingers to run through her hair as he kissed her.

* * *

May squeezed her thighs around Ben and ran her hands through his hair. His cologne had a cinnamon and citrus scent that drove her mad. His thick tufts of hair beneath her finger tips also pushed May over the edge of desire. She wasn't sure what had come over her — what had possessed her to leap into Ben's arms. She knew nothing about him, but her body propelled her forward like this.

Thud.

Ben carried May to another wall and pressed her up against the wall as he kissed her lips and neck.

"I can't wait to take you upstairs and fuck your brains out," He whispered.

***

May was taken aback by the dirty talk. It wasn't typical for guys that she'd just met to go that far on the first night. But coming from Ben, she felt her pussy getting wet. That was exactly what she wanted from him. Ben set May on the ground and then turned her around, pressing her against the wall.

"Before I fuck you upstairs, I'm going to pin you down and fuck you against this wall until you scream."

May did nothing to resist. She pressed her hands against the wall and stuck her ass out. Ben hiked her skirt up and slid her underwear to the ground.

"Mmm," He groaned when he saw May's

perfect, large ass.

Her butt cheeks were large, round and juicy. May jiggled her ass cheeks a little, tantalizing Ben and activating his desires for her further. He rubbed the area of May's ass cheeks and felt his cock stirring to attention. For a woman with such a slim waist, May's butt was deliciously large.

Ben got down on his knees and grabbed May's thighs.

"Don't turn around," He commanded, "Just feel."

May closed her eyes, waiting for what was coming next. She expected to feel Ben's member sliding towards her pussy, but instead, she felt the warm wetness of Ben's tongue touch the soft area between her legs.

"Ahh," May moaned.

She had no idea what she was in for. Ben squeezed her thighs tighter and began to move his tongue smoothly across the length of her pussy.

"Yes! Oh yes…" May cooed.

Ben began to lap at her pussy faster and faster. His lips suckled around May's engorged clit as he licked the length of her pussy, even allowing his tongue to dare graze her puckered asshole.

"Ohhh!" May cried out as his tongue grazed against the forbidden hole again.

* * *

Ben stood up and then pressed May into the wall further with his body.

"Stay still," He whispered, "I'm going to fuck you now."

May remained still and she could hear Ben undoing his pants. She could feel the heat of his cock pressing up against her ass cheeks as he kissed the back of her neck and shoulders.

"Condom?" May asked.

"Yes," Ben replied.

As he answered her, he shoved the full length of his sheathed cock into her wetness. May let out a loud squeal. Ben began to pummel into her pussy. He gripped her waist and fucked her against the wall, right there in her foyer. May began to cry out louder and louder as she felt her body approaching climax.

When Ben's cock first slid inside her pussy he felt incredibly huge — bigger than any guy she'd been with. Now, May struggled to accommodate each powerful thrust. He was pounding into her harder and harder. Her pussy juiced with each thrust and May found herself gasping and gasping until she reached release.

"Ohhh yess!" May cried out as she came.

Feeling her tightness grabbing onto his cock like a vice, Ben pulled out of her.

"Take me upstairs," He demanded.

* * *

May turned around and caught a glimpse of the monster cock Ben was packing. His lust muscle was even bigger than she'd envisioned it. She couldn't wait to impale herself on his dick again and allow herself stronger and stronger climaxes than ever before.

May led Ben upstairs to her bedroom. She saw the look of animalistic desire in his eyes. She saw that he wanted her more than everything and that he'd been hunting her from the moment he'd seen her. May had to admit to herself that it felt good to be a prize to a man like Ben. He could have had any girl in the room but he'd chosen her — the klutz that had caused a public scene at a fancy restaurant.

Once in the bedroom, May turned to face him

with a smile on her face.

"Wow... You're... really big," She said.

Ben grinned, "Oh yeah? Never noticed."

"Funny."

"Turn around sweetheart before you lose a chance to experience all of this."

"I think I'll need help getting out of these clothes," May teased.

Ben rushed to her and unzipped her dress. He stripped it off of her and then unhooked her bra. For the first time, he caught a glimpse of May fully nude and his cock twitched to attention again.

* * *

May turned away from him and positioned herself on all fours like he'd demanded. With baby hairs slicked to her head with sweat and makeup running off her face, May found herself desperate for another climax. She felt Ben climb into the bed behind her. She felt his warm, large hands running all over her flesh and then she felt his cock lining up with her tightness.

"Ready baby?"

"Mmhmm," May whimpered. Ben shoved the full length of his cock into her with one stroke.

May cried out and Ben continued to pound into her harder and harder. He felt himself coming close to climax, close to claiming this beautiful dark-skinned beauty as his own. May moaned and cried out as she came; she thrust her hips back against Ben as she writhed in orgasm. Unable to contain himself a second longer, Ben grunted and emptied himself into the condom that separated their flesh.

He squeezed May's hips as he came and then slowly removed his long member from her tightness. They both gasped for breath, high from the intensity of the climaxes between them.

2 Bound

Ben had disappeared for a week. After their night together, the morning had passed in a whirlwind. May sat on her front porch with a black tea as she thought back to the week prior. In the morning, she'd caught Ben trying to sneak out. He'd been awkward — different from the night before.

"This was fun."

"I may call you again if I'm bored and horny."

May toyed those phrases over and over again in her mind. They sounded suspiciously calloused for the man that had behaved as if they had some deep, special connection just the night before. Before May could gather her bearings, of course Ben had just left. She had no answers — just an intense night of passion and a deep peach pit of shame in her belly.

May regretted jumping into bed with Ben now. She hadn't expected a lifetime of love, but she at least thought he'd be willing to give her a chance, not just relegate her to a lifetime of "maybe if I'm bored and horny".

After tea, May had gone to work. She had a half-day, and returned home in the early afternoon. May checked her phone, and listened to the voicemail from Kristin again. Right — thirty minutes until her best friend arrived. May took a quick shower, put a kettle on for some nice hot tea and then got dressed.

Kristin arrived on time, using her key to May's house to let herself in.

* * *

"May! May I'm here!"

May bounded down the stairs and wrapped Kristin in a large hug.

"How the hell is my bride to be?"

"She's wonderful," Kristin spoke, with a sparkle in her voice that had become a part of her aura ever since her engagement.

"Well lucky you."

"What's going on with you? You never told me how that date with Khalil ended!"

May rolled her eyes and shook her head, remembering the date with Khalil that had been doomed to fail from the start.

* * *

"Ugh," May sighed, "It was awful."

"What was wrong with him?"

"He was just... gross," May said.

She didn't feel like mentioning Khalil's gross comment about bed wenches to Kristin; she didn't think Kristin would really understand all the implications that went into that comment anyways.

"Wait," Kristin paused, "You said you went home with someone though. That wasn't Khalil?"

May shook her head and wrinkled her nose in disgust.

***

"No. It wasn't."

"Oh my goodness, you met someone else?!" Kristin said.

Her eyes were alight with excitement. Since her engagement, single friends' escapades had become an addictive drug to Kristin. Her anxiety about getting married carried over into her social life and made Kristin desperate to share in every sordid detail of her single friends' experiences.

"I guess you could say that," May offered.

"Tell me all about him!"

May felt heat rising to her face. She didn't know

how to talk about Ben without feeling embarrassed. When May had mentioned him to Kristin, she'd expected he'd be scheduling a first (or second?) date, not ignoring her for a week straight.

"He was okay…"

"Something's going on," Kristin said, folding her arms.

May hung her head and then muttered, "He hasn't call me back."

"So what? It's not like you slept with him!" Kristin chipped.

May looked at her guiltily.

* * *

"Uh oh."

"Yeah."

"You slept with him on the first date?" Kristin replied, trying to hide her shock.

May shrugged, "If you could call it date."

"May!" Kristin chastised, "This is so unlike you! What happened?"

"I don't know what happened. But he's an asshole, so let's just move on from it."

"Yeah," Kristin said, "He is an asshole if he didn't call you back. But was he cute…"

May groaned.

* * *

"Kristin!" May chided her, "I already feel like enough of an idiot for even giving this guy the time of day. The last thing I want to think about is whether or not he's cute.

"Aww please!" Kristin begged.

May smirked, "Well he was cute enough for me to forget my morals for a night."

Kristin giggled, "I can't believe this. The one guy who you let down your walls for ends up being a total asshole."

"Just my luck, right?" May replied.

"If he doesn't want to date you, he's worthless anyways."

"Thanks for the vote of confidence."

"I'm serious!" Kristin assured her.

"And I appreciate it. You've always been my number one."

Kristin peered around May's shoulder and wrinkled her nose.

"What?" May asked.

"Uhh," Kristin said, "Are you expecting anyone?"

"No…"

"Turn around. I think you have a visitor."

* * *

May turned around and felt a lump in her throat as she saw a white BMW parked in her driveway.

"Ohmygoodness."

"Is that him?" Kristin asked, her eyes widened in delight at the opportunity to watch this drama unfold before her very eyes.

"Yes, that's him," May whispered, "What the hell is he doing here?"

"Looks like he's come to make up for not calling."

Kristin and May kept their eyes glued to the window, where they saw Ben approaching with a bouquet of white peonies that looked *ginormous*. He was dressed well too. May could feel the lump in her throat growing harder as she noticed how *sexy* he was in this outfit, with his car, and wielding a bouquet of perfect flowers.

"Maybe the sex was better than you realized," Kristin teased, "It drove him crazy."

"What do I do Kristin?!" May panicked, "I look awful! I'm in no place to meet him right now! I'm brooding!"

Kristin chuckled, "Oh hush. I'll sneak out the back door and you just stay here to meet him."

"Are you sure?" May asked, "We're supposed to be having a girl's day."

* * *

Kristin waved May off, "Come on, you haven't been with a guy in *years*. I can't let you pass up this opportunity."

Ouch. Kristin had a point though.

Kristin slunk out the back door. May turned towards the front door, where she could see Ben waiting, his hand hovering over her doorbell.

May opened her door before he could ring it.

"Ben. What are you doing here?"

She didn't mean to sound so testy, but she just couldn't help it. She'd felt totally pathetic waiting for Ben to just call or text her back. In typical male fashion, just when she'd given up on him, he'd returned for more. And this time, he'd arrived with bribes.

"I brought you flowers," He said.

"Thanks."

May took the flowers from Ben and moved to close the door.

"May! Wait, I brought you something else."

Ben took a step into her house. May would have protested about his uninvited entry, but she saw the box he was carrying in his hands had a *very* nice label on it.

"What's that?"

"I thought that would get your attention," Ben

grinned.

"You know what. Never mind. Thanks for the flowers, why don't you head out now."

Ben continued to grin, like he was privy to some information that May wasn't.

"Open it. You know you want to."

May took the box from him, but she didn't lose her hesitation completely. She opened the box and gasped at the contents.

"Ben! What is this? Why did you get me this?"

May pulled the dress out of the box. The dress was the exact shade of brown as her skin and made out of silk that was incredibly soft to the touch. Along with the dress was a string of pearls with such brilliance that May couldn't help but lust after putting them on immediately. This wasn't the sort of person she was usually — the type that could be bought with gifts — but what Ben brought her was the best gift she'd ever received. It was certainly the most expensive one.

"I don't know if I can take this," May said worriedly.

"You must," Ben said, in his soothing low voice, "I want you to put them on immediately. We're going out."

May scoffed, "Right now? We're going out right now?"

* * *

"Yes," Ben replied, "I can give you a few minutes to change."

"You can't just waltz into people's lives like this and..."

"And expect them to have the best night of their lives?" Ben interrupted, "Hurry up before I find someone else to put in that dress."

May snatched the box even further away from him and then began to run upstairs. She bounded up the stairs into her bedroom and then took a look at the contents of the box again. The pearls were gorgeous, and according to the tag on them, they weren't man-made. Meaning, they were even rarer than any pearls May had of her own. The silk dress looked beautiful, but May was almost scared to put it on.

* * *

She took a quick shower and then brushed out her hair, flat ironing her tresses into silky waves. May stood before her mirror nude and then slipped the pearls around her neck. The brilliant white balls stood out against her dark skin. May felt that her skin was luminous, glowing with a depth of rich color that emanated her light outwards. It was time for the dress. May couldn't believe how easily she was succumbing to Ben's wishes and desires, but something about him felt so *right*. The way he commanded her attention was the closest May had experienced to hypnosis.

She slipped the dress on and gasped. May had never worn something like this out of the house. Even standing in her bedroom before her mirror, she felt exposed. May typically dressed in a stylish yet conservative manner. This dress hugged all her curves and showed everything. The hem of the dress fell to her mid thighs, stretching tightly over her bodacious buttocks.

"I don't know if I can do this," May muttered to herself.

She turned around a few times in the mirror, ogling her body and wondering if there was some way she could cover up just a little bit more.

"Tick tock May!"

She heard Ben's voice calling to her from downstairs. He was dominant — and demanding — and not an easy person for her to say no to. May turned from side to side in the mirror again.

Her nipples poked out through the front of the dress. The way the silk draped over her tits felt comfortable on her skin, but to go *out* like this? May didn't think she really had it in her.

But it was another date with Ben. She'd spent all week pining over him and mourning the fact that he'd tossed her aside as soon as he'd gotten laid. Getting him back into her home felt like a victory. May knew she'd feel foolish if she tossed it aside.

"Coming!" She replied.

She slipped into heels — she knew Ben wanted her in heels — and then walked downstairs where she saw him waiting impatiently for her arrival. His gaze shifted from frustration to adulation the moment he saw her in the dress.

May could already imagine all the naughty things he wanted to do to her.

"Wow," He mumbled.

For once, Ben was at a loss for words.

"This is… a lot," May said.

"A whole lot of beauty," Ben replied with a grin.

May rolled her eyes. Ben continued to stare at her, unfazed by her attitude.

"Let's get out of here."

She hesitated.

* * *

"I don't know if I can leave the house wearing this."

She saw a flash of disappointment on Ben's face, then his resolve only stiffened, "You can. Trust me."

May turned around, giving Ben a full view of her body. She could see him undressing her with his eyes.

"Don't make me wait any longer or we may never get out of this house tonight."

"Fine," May said, "You've won me over this time. But it won't be so easy next time."

Ben smirked, "Who says it won't."

* * *

"You're insufferable, you know that?" May replied.

But sure enough, she walked towards the door and followed Ben to his BMW. The magnetic pull towards him was that strong. May found that her desire for Ben was unnatural. He was the kind of guy who wouldn't call her for a week, but she found herself chasing after his affections.

In the car, May started to grow comfortable in the deep ochre silk dress. Ben reached over and squeezed her thighs as they drove. As his skin touched hers, May couldn't help but recall the first night of passion between them. And now, they were going on their first real date.

Ben started speeding down the highway and

May wondered where they were going, but she didn't want to ask. She didn't think Ben would tell her anyways. Ben squeezed her thigh and spoke first, "So. Did you miss me?"

"Miss you?" May laughed.

She hated to say that she did. She hated missing the feeling of being absolutely possessed by Ben. She missed the feeling of his kisses and the opportunity to get to know him better.

"You totally missed me," Ben said.

May felt heat rising to her face. She didn't want Ben to know that despite the fact that he'd been an asshole, she was developing something close to *feelings* for him.

* * *

"I didn't," May asserted, "And you're mighty sure of yourself for a one-night stand."

"One night stand?" Ben replied confused, "That's not what this is all about."

Now May was really confused. Ben had left her with the impression that this was casual — totally casual.

"Well then what *is* this about?"

Maybe this would be the chance to pin down answers from her elusive rescuer. On one level, she barely knew Ben, but they'd already slept together and the connection they'd built that night made May feel like she'd known him for years.

* * *

Ben tried to skirt past her question, "Just have fun May… You're a beautiful woman and I love a good time with a beautiful woman."

"That's it?"

"Does it have to be more than that?"

May said nothing. When Ben stopped the car, May looked around, trying to figure out where they were exactly.

"We're here."

"Where?"

They were on a hill, but the place was isolated. There was no restaurant, no nightclub. Really, May had dressed up for Ben and Ben alone.

*　*　*

"I have something to show you. I'll come 'round and get your door."

May waited for Ben to come around and then he opened the car door and led her out. Her heels sank gently into the earth as she walked around to the front of the car. Ben leaned up against his BMW with his arms folded and looked out over the horizon.

"Beautiful, isn't it?"

They were just outside of the city, parked on a hill overlooking the view below.

"Yes, it's gorgeous," May said.

A wind picked up and she started to feel chilly.

May used her hands to rub herself warm.

"Here, take my jacket," Ben said.

He took his jacket off and draped it over May's shoulders.

"This is one of my favorite places in the city," Ben started, "This is where I come to think… and unwind… and tonight, I want to show you something."

May turned to look at him, "What is it?"

Before Ben could answer, May looked to the sky and saw an exploding pink firework bursting over a horizon. The boom of the fireworks followed as the pink sparkles started raining down to the ground. Before May could react, another firework exploded in the air. May let out a shriek and watched fascinated as the sparkly flames fell from the sky.

Two, three more fireworks went off and May stood mesmerized, watching the show before her. Ben had really organized all of this just for her. Ben moved in closer and wrapped his arms around May. She nestled into his arms and they watched the rest of the fireworks show in silence. Ben's warm arms held May tightly and she felt the electricity fizzling between them with just the gentlest touch.

Ben pushed her hair aside and whispered into her ear, "This is for you beautiful... This is how you made me feel from the first moment I met you."

May felt dizzy with excitement. Ben leaned over and kissed her cheek. May felt heat rising to her chest. She reached over and squeezed Ben's hand. He squeezed her hand back.
"Do you like the show?" He asked as the fireworks began to fizzle out.

"Yes," May replied, "This was so lovely."

"Not as lovely as you are," Ben whispered.

They turned to each other and Ben planted his lips against May's. She succumbed to his kisses and wondered what Ben was playing at here. She could sense that he liked her, but there was no sense as to how deep his affections really went.

May pulled away and looked into Ben's green

eyes. They were fixated on her with fervent desire.

"I want to get to know you May. I know I'm a complicated man, but it's clear we have a connection. I want to do everything in my power to explore that."

May leaned her head against Ben's shoulders and rested there for a few minutes. Then they started talking. Their conversation went on for hours. May found herself opening up to Ben in a way she hadn't opened up to anyone in a long time. And for all his masculine posturing, Ben could be sweet. He was a good listener. Staring into his green eyes, May felt like she could say anything in the world without judgment.

And of course, there was the physical attraction

that made her blood run red hot through her veins. He awakened a desire inside May that had been dormant. And as much as she knew she should pull back, May found herself mesmerized.

The evening was passing on, and the lights in the buildings below began to dim as the city's residents slipped into the deep resonant sleep of late night slumber. May had promised herself that she wouldn't go home with Ben tonight.

But it was getting harder to say no to him. May felt the strong pull he exerted on her and she wanted to say "no" again. If she didn't say no, May feared that she'd permanently be relegated to the role of a "friend with benefits". But that wasn't what she wanted from Ben. She wanted them to connect like this — over long evening conversations and jazz music.

* * *

"What's on your mind?" Ben whispered.

He grazed his tongue along May's neck and then kissed her. She pulled away from him, convinced that she could resist the urge to jump into bed with him again.

May giggled, "That I'm not going home with you tonight."

Ben pulled away and raised an eyebrow, "Is that what you think?"

"Yes," May said, "It's what I know. I won't just hop into bed whenever you ask me to."

Ben leaned over and kissed May's neck again.

* * *

"Why not?"

"Because…" May mumbled as Ben kissed her neck again, totally distracting her from the point she was going to make.

She pulled away from him again, "Because you can't just have whatever you want whenever you want it."

"Why not…" Ben replied.

This time, he didn't just kiss May's neck. He kissed her on the lips, long and slow and deep. May closed her eyes and allowed Ben to kiss her. She felt the tingling from her skin race down her back. The hairs on the back of her neck stood up and she felt wetness between her legs.

* * *

This wasn't supposed to happen. She was supposed to be *resisting* him. Not this.

May pulled away again.

"Ben... Stop. You need to take me home..."

"If I take you home," Ben whispered, "It will only be so I can pin you to your bed and fuck you all night long."

Fuck. May hated how quickly he turned her on. The naughtier he was and the more persistent he was, the more May found herself succumbing to him. He wanted her badly and he wasn't going to take "no" for an answer — she knew that. And as much as she wanted to resist him, deep down, May wanted him too. She wanted to feel his hard thing between her legs. She wanted to feel him pinning her down and taking control of her body like he owned her.

But still… There had to be at least one last ditch effort to resist him.

"You'll take me home and you'll drop me off… That's what you're gonna do."

Ben smirked. He didn't believe her — and she hardly believed herself.

"Fine," He said, "I'll take you home. And I'll leave you right at the door."

May's heart was racing as he agreed. Perhaps she'd won after all. Perhaps she'd actually succeeded in resisting Ben's arrogant, dominant advances — the advances she knew *should* repel her but were really having the opposite effect. May found herself even hungrier for Ben's touch, and even hungrier for Ben's lips against her own lips, against her neck and against her breasts.

Ben opened the door for her and helped May into the front seat. Ben started to drive. He was driving fast — heading quickly towards May's home. Ben had no intention of leaving May at the door, but for now, he'd let her think that she'd gotten what she wanted.

As he drove, Ben's hand squeezed May's thigh. The silk from her dress brushed up against his hand. Ben could already feel himself getting hard. As they sped down the highway, May shifted uncomfortably in her seat. Ben was going fast — really fast. At first, May's heart was beating out of her chest. But as she settled down, she started to really enjoy the speed.

When Ben pulled off the road towards her house, a different feeling overcame May. It was a mixture of anxiety and self-doubt. Her body wanted her to succumb to Ben's desires and submit to his commands. But her mind was telling her to do the opposite. Her mind was telling her to refuse him and enter into another game of cat-and-mouse to keep him interested.

Ben parked in front of May's house and turned to her with a grin.

"Are you going to stop playing hard to get or should I drop you off and drive away from here."

* * *

May turned to Ben and bit down on her lower lip, unsure of what to say.

"You're a bastard, you know that?" May whispered.

Ben smirked and then placed his finger under May's chin, drawing her gaze to his.

"If I'm such a bastard, why do you want me so damn badly?"

May didn't have an answer to his question. She couldn't explain why she wanted Ben so badly. There was nothing logical about her feelings for him and nothing logical about how strong their connection had been so fast. And it wasn't just about what was happening in the bedroom. It was about the way he'd helped her out of a pinch from the moment he'd met her. It was about the way he'd taken her to the top of a distant hill and arranged a giant fireworks show for her. It was about the way he listened to her without interrupting, interested in what she had to say.

Of course, there was plenty wrong with Ben. He was too suave, too dominant, too unwilling to take no for an answer. But damn, he was hot. He had the most gorgeous green eyes and a perfect body. He knew how to handle a woman in bed and he knew how to make her cum over and over again.

"I have no clue," May whispered.

And then she leaned over and kissed Ben. Heck,

she could have him right here if he wanted to. May reached over where Ben was sitting in his car and felt his cock through his pants. He was rock hard.

"We should go inside," May said.

"No," Ben demanded, "We'll go to mine."

Ben nodded, pleased that he'd won. May knew she'd failed to resist Ben, but she couldn't stop herself from going forward with this. Ben sped off, and they drove towards his house. May had never been to Ben's place and she didn't have time to care about how dangerous it was. After the evening they'd had together, she felt safe with him. He might be a calloused asshole every once in a while, but he was safe.

* * *

When they arrived at Ben's place, May didn't have time to process. His house was *huge* and that stuck out to May, but aside from that, she was too distracted to notice too many other details. The car had revealed that Ben was wealthy, but May was just beginning to find out just how wealthy he was.

It was intimidating. But Ben wouldn't allow her the time to be intimidated. He was driven towards the single purpose of getting her into bed and May knew now wasn't the time to ask him questions — like why his red brick mansion looked like it could house a small army.

The next thing May knew they were inside and locked in each other's arms. Each kiss was followed by another. May could feel her pussy getting wetter and wetter.

* * *

Ben grabbed her ass through the silk dress, enjoying the way his prize for the night looked with the brown silk clinging to her curves and highlighting all of her sexiest features.

"I want you so badly," Ben grunted.

He squeezed May's ass, causing her to squeal. Ben's cock grew harder with excitement as he thought about what he wanted to approach May with that night. The first time he'd climbed into bed with her, he was testing the waters and tonight, he would see how much May could handle.

Ben pulled away from their ardent kisses.

"May," He said, "I have something to ask you."

"What is it?"

"It's a confession."

Now May was beyond curious. What could Ben possibly want to confess to her that would be worth interrupting their night of passion.

"Tell me," She urged.

"When I'm with you… I want to be myself. I want to explore certain things in the bedroom — certain things that may scare you."

"That may scare me?" May asked with concern.

Ben held her hands and pressed them towards his lips.

* * *

"Yes," He said, "Many women don't have what it takes to satisfy all my proclivities."

"What kind of proclivities…"

Ben shrugged, "I'm a very kinky man."

"How kinky?"

"We don't have to get that deep tonight. We can start lightly," Ben said, kissing her palms again. May could tell that he was still observing her, gauging her reaction and trying to figure out if he'd gone too far.

May still couldn't tell what Ben meant. She had a sense of how kinky he could get — he was dominant and he loved the feeling of her pressed up against the wall submitting to his very desires. But how far could this encounter really go? How much was Ben willing to put her through?

"I don't know…"

Ben dropped her hands and his face took on a stern expression, "Well, you must agree. And you must be sure of what you want. Otherwise, I'll walk out of here and that will be the end of this."

May could tell that he was serious now. And now, Ben hadn't just gotten her pussy wet. He had activated her mind and her head was spinning imagining all the naughty things she could let him do to her.

* * *

"Fine. I agree."

"Are you sure?"

May nodded, "Yes. I agree."

"Good."

Ben took her into his arms again and this time when he kissed her, his hand snaked up towards her throat. He grasped her throat as they kissed but he didn't squeeze. Ben displayed his power and let her know that he *could* do anything — but he wouldn't without her permission.

Ben pulled away, "If you don't like what happens here tonight, you never have to see me again."

* * *

May nodded. She could feel her arms and legs trembling slightly. A mixture of anticipation and fear clouded her mind. All she could do was submit to him.

"Let's go to my bedroom."

Ben led May to his bedroom — a giant room with a king-sized bed in the middle. Above the king-sized bed was a mirror. Ben clapped his hands upon entering the room and blue lights illuminated the space. He clapped his hands again and a low throbbing techno sounded throughout the room.

Ben closed the door behind them and locked it.

"Strip," He commanded.

* * *

May was starting to see his playboy side again. Ben could be a charming gentleman in the streets, but she could tell he was about to get nastier than ever between the sheets.

But she obeyed.

May slipped the silk dress onto the ground and stood before Ben with no bra, lace panties and the pearls that he'd gifted to her earlier that night. He smirked when he saw her gorgeous body presented to him like a gift and adorned with the pearls that he'd given to her. May was especially attuned to his desires.

"You look hot," Ben said.

May didn't respond. She felt the heat rushing to her face and mild discomfort at standing before

Ben like she was a piece of meat to be analyzed, poked and prodded.

"Put your hands behind your back."

May did as she was told and placed her hands behind her back. She stood still while Ben moved to a large mahogany dresser. He opened up the second drawer and pulled out thick black ropes. May's pussy throbbed as she saw the ropes. It didn't take a genius to figure out what was coming next. But this time, instead of fear, May felt indescribable desire.

Ben began to bind her wrists behind her back. May waited for him to tie the knots, letting him know when they were just right. Ben finished his handiwork.

* * *

"Try to move," He instructed.

May tried to move her hands apart or wriggle out of the binds, but she was stuck. Ben's bondage was enough to restrict her movements.

"Good," Ben said, "Now walk towards the bed and get on all fours."

May moved slowly towards the bed. Without the use of her hands, she tried to get on "all fours". Her face pressed into the soft mattress and her back arched, exposing her ass and pussy for Ben's pleasure.

"Very good," Ben said gently, "Now, I'll bind your legs."

May's heart began to beat out of her chest.

Bound hands were one thing, but with both her arms and legs bound, she'd be at Ben's mercy completely. He could use her as he wished and she'd have no recourse except to cry out in pain.

Their connection was such that it was almost like Ben could read her mind.

"Fear not," He said.

Ben returned to the dresser and emerged with another set of ropes. May couldn't see a thing at this point, but she could feel Ben move across the room and then she could feel his hands grabbing her legs and securing them together. The ropes weren't painful; that didn't make May nervous. What made her nervous was not knowing what was coming next. What made her nervous was trusting a man like Ben without *really* knowing whether or not he'd hurt her.

There was risk involved.

"We need a safe word," He said, once May was good and tied.

"Oh…"

May's innocence when it came to his kinky proclivities turned Ben on even more than her body. See, it wasn't just her body and her beautiful brown skin Ben was attracted to. There was more about her that drove him crazy. It was something about the way she laughed, the way she wrinkled up her nose when she thought he was being a dick, the way she could open up to him and talk for hours at a time without tiring.

* * *

"The safe word is going to be 'bananas'."

"Bananas?"

"Use it only if you can't take it anymore."

"Yes," May nodded.

Ben cringed. She was rough around the edges still but this was just the beginning of training her. In this situation "yes" wouldn't do. It had to be "yes sir".

"In the future, address me as sir whenever we are in this bedroom. Do you understand?"

"Yes, sir."

"Good."

*   *   *

"Now remain here while I get ready."

Ben stripped down to nothing and ogled the gorgeous woman on his bed. May didn't just have a beautiful body, she had the sexiest pussy and asshole — two parts of her he couldn't wait to possess. May had a hairless, tight butthole and plump velvety pussy lips which were also hairless. Ben didn't just want to sleep with her, he wanted to tongue her precious folds until she was screaming and begging for mercy.

That would have to wait for another night. Naked and fully erect, Ben positioned himself behind May on the bed. He shuddered as his hand touched her soft plump ass cheeks. He was too eager to enter her for him to wait another second.

* * *

Ben rolled a rubber onto his dick and then began to press his hardness deep between May's folds. He went slowly allowing himself to enjoy diving into every inch of her tightness.

"OHHH," May squealed as Ben's tumescent cock pushed past her hardness.

Ben squeezed her hips and slid his full length all the way inside her pussy. May found herself wanting to brace her body against the bed, but she couldn't. The restraints around her arms and legs were too secure.

Ben began to drive his cock between her legs with a steady rhythm. He began to pump his hardness between her legs hard and fast. May's pussy was entirely slick as he pounded his dick deeper and deeper. She began to moan loudly and Ben could tell she would climax quickly — and repeatedly.

With each thrust, May's head was pushed into the bed. She craved this sense of deep submission and once Ben had unlocked that craving she felt free to cum… and to cum… and to cum…

May let out a loud cry as her pussy exploded with pleasure. Her core was fired up with lust and each thrust set forth a chain reaction that led to a bigger and bigger climax. Ben gripped her ass tightly and began to ram his cock in harder and faster. The more he watched May writhe desperately for her freedom beneath him, the more he wanted to finish inside her.

*** * *

May couldn't handle the intensity of each powerful orgasm. Her head was spinning and stars sparked behind her eyes as Ben continued to thrust into her.

Ben grunted and he started grunted like a strong animal as he edged closer towards a release of his own. Just before cumming, he took his thumb and began to massage May's perfect asshole as he thrust and thrust into her pussy. In a final moan, May reached the last climax she could handle. She shuddered and her sensitive pussy ached with each repeated thrust.

There had been no need for a safe word. In fact, May hardly wanted the night to end.

"Please…" She whimpered.

* * *

Ben ignored her, but only because he would have cum without her begging. He let out a loud groan as he released a large load of cum between May's legs. They both shuddered together, experiencing the aftershocks of their releases in unison, until the aftershocks subsided, leaving a feeling of cool euphoria behind.

Ben pulled out of May and tossed the condom in the trash. Now, he had to release his prize from her binds, and see what pleasures she could bring him next.

3 Mercy

After a night of continuous pleasure, May woke up the next morning unsure of how she got there. For a brief moment, she forgot where she was and a sharp pang of panic gripped her chest. She slowly started to piece together the events of the previous night. It had started off moping with Kristin, but the events had kicked off when Ben had surprised her with a sexy brown silk dress.

Damn that dress. That dress had awakened something inside May and caused her to forget her promise to herself to pull back from this addictive "situation" with Ben. It wasn't a relationship. They were bonded, but there was no label or explicit concept of how deep that bond really went.

May just knew that she was hooked. Ben was

beyond charming and in the bedroom, she'd never experienced that much pleasure in her life. It was dizzying to keep up with and even more dizzying for her to try to make sense of. There was nothing sensible about their interaction, which was against everything that had ever happened in May's life. She had *always* been sensible until Ben.

She turned over in bed and saw that Ben was gone. Great. May sat up and surveyed the room properly for the first time. Drunk on desire the night before, she'd hardly noticed the fact that Ben's house reminded her of a castle. His bedroom was massive, with ornate chandeliers, blue mood lighting along the walls, a built in surround sound system, and brand new mahogany furniture with craftsmanship that bested anything she'd seen in a chain store.

* * *

May sat up in bed and propped her body up with two of Ben's soft, down pillows. She pulled the down comforter over her body and tried to figure out where her clothes from the night before had gone. May surveyed the room from bed but saw no sign of the silk dress. Or her shoes. Apparently, Ben had removed them. Great — she was stuck here completely naked.

May inched out of bed towards Ben's walk in closet and she searched for something she could wear. May settled on a cerulean blue oxford that was way too big for her and fit her like an oversized dress. May slipped into the shirt and buttoned it up, leaving a couple buttons undone. She returned to Ben's bed and lay back again, taking it all in.

* * *

Ben had to be ridiculously rich. Owning a single restaurant was profitable, but May didn't think it would make Ben this ridiculously rich. May was startled by a knock on the door to Ben's bedroom.

"Cleaning! May I come in!"

May was startled. A cleaning service?

"Uhh sure!"

The door opened and a woman walked in. She was Southeast Asian, with soft tawny skin and long black hair, braided in a perfect single braid down the center of her back. She was older than May — but not by too much — and dressed in a crisp white maid's uniform.

* * *

"Good morning!" She said with cheer, "I'm Annie. Stay comfortable and let me know if you need anything. I'll just be tidying the bathroom and then I'll get you breakfast in bed."

"Good morning," May replied, "And thank you Annie. My name's May."

Annie smiled in response, but May got the impression that she wasn't keen on making friends. Annie tidied up the bathroom and then came out, facing May in bed again.

"For breakfast, do you have any allergies or food specifications miss?"

May felt uncomfortable being addressed as *miss* by someone who was older than her, but she felt that it would be even more uncomfortable to upset Annie's equilibrium. She told Annie that she had no food allergies and waited for Ben's housekeeper to bustle off. The housekeeper, breakfast in bed, and the mansion were all throwing May off.

Not to mention, she had no clue where Ben was.

May pulled out her phone and considered calling Kristin. But again, how would she explain this to Kristin? Kristin had bigger problems. She was planning her wedding and preparing for her new life. The last thing she'd want to hear about was May's inability to stay out of Ben Hawthorne's bed.

May didn't bother calling. But she wasn't left alone for long. Annie returned pushing a gilded tray with a breakfast spread that she left at

May's bedside.

"Excuse me," May asked before Annie left the room, "Do you know when Ben will be back?"

"Mr. Hawthorne?"

May nodded.

"He will be back shortly. Enjoy your breakfast."

Great. Annie hadn't been much help in figuring out where Ben was, but May figured that the least she could do was to eat her breakfast without much complaint. She poured herself a glass of orange juice as Annie left the room. There was coffee, orange juice, slice fruit, croissants, salted meats as well as cheese and crackers.

***

May drank a glass of orange juice and then dug into the fruit. She was nearly done sampling everything on the tray when Ben pushed open the doors to his bedroom and greeted her with a deep-bellied good morning.

"Good morning," May replied.

"Did you enjoy breakfast?"

May nodded. The coffee had certainly helped but she was still slowly easing into the day.

"Yes, it was lovely. And I met Annie."

Ben smiled, "Oh yes, Annie. She's been working with me for years."

***

"She's sweet. And she makes a damn good breakfast," May replied.

Ben smiled and then rested his hand on May's thigh.

"Well I expect you'll be wanting to leave soon."

"Leave?" May looked at him confused.

"Well it's morning. Staying any later would make this... weird."

Again, May was thrust into that confusing state with Ben again. He was constantly flip flopping on what he wanted. And now that they'd had this *insane* night together, it sounded like Ben wanted to push her away again. Only this time, May wouldn't let him.

*　*　*

"I don't think it would make it weird," May asserted.

Ben looked at her with curiosity. His green eyes were blazing with excitement for the challenge May was presenting to him. He loved watching her go from reluctant to pursuant.

"So you want to stay?"

May shrugged, "I guess."

"I can see it in your eyes. You want to be here. Was it something about last night?"

Was it? May remembered how it felt to be tied up and at Ben's mercy entirely. Of course something about that felt amazing. She craved another encounter with him just as intense as the one the night before. She didn't care if it was morning. She didn't care if Ben got more intense with her. She just wanted him.

"Yes I want to be here."

Ben leaned over and kissed her, "Let me guess, the precious good girl actually enjoyed being tied up."

May looked down bashfully. It was still hard growing accustomed to how brazen Ben was.

"Well fine," Ben acquiesced, "You can stay. But if you stay, I'll want you to fulfill my every need."

"And what kinds of needs might those be?" May

asked.

She already had in mind what Ben might ask of her. May knew that Ben could get more intense, even insane with the level of domination he required. But this morning, she was willing to submit. Whether or not she wanted to admit it to herself, she was getting hooked on his arrogance and entranced by his personality.

"Any and everything," Ben replied with a grin.

He stood up and then gestured towards the door, "Let me inform Annie that you're finished with breakfast and I'll be back in a few minutes."

Ben left the room for a while and May sat in bed nervous. The wetness between her thighs was still sore from the hard pounding the night before. Despite that, she felt desperate to feel his hardness between her thighs again. May was developing an insatiable appetite for the sort of powerful earth-shattering orgasms like what she experienced with Ben.

Annie came in and they exchanged a few words as she cleared breakfast. May found Annie beautiful and also noticed that she was happy. May wasn't altogether comfortable with the idea of "help". But Annie seemed happy and May could envision herself having a life where everything was just a tad bit easier — that's what a life with Ben would promise.

As soon as the thought popped into her head, May wanted to smack herself. There was no life with Ben. Ben was a free spirit — he'd made that clear. She could hardly pin him down for more than a night. No matter how connected they were, May knew it would be her best bet to keep focused on the present. Ben wasn't the sort of man interested in a future.

When he returned, May found herself resentful of how much she wanted him. Whatever he had in store for her would be good punishment.

Ben closed his bedroom door and without much introduction began, "Are you ready for things to become more intense?"

May didn't know if she was ready, but she agreed anyways.

"Yes. I'm ready."

"Last night went well," Ben said.

* * *

His voice was changing into that cool, controlling voice he used when his desires were starting to magnify.

"Yes," May agreed, "It went well."

"This morning, I want to start slow with some more light bondage. After you've cum until you can't walk, we'll move onto more."

May nodded.

"Are you ready?"

"I think so," May replied.

"Perfect," Ben finished, "Now get into the shower and I'll join you. We need to clean off."

May got up out of bed with just Ben's shirt that she'd stolen from his closet. When he saw her wearing his shirt his cock jumped. Ben desperately wanted to suppress the reaction but the truth was, he was turned on every time he got the notion of possessing May completely. He had her affection, but he wanted more than just her infatuation — he wanted her complete devotion.

Of course, there was a major problem with her devotion that Ben couldn't get past. If May devoted herself to him, she'd want the same thing in return. Ben didn't know if he could give her that yet. He'd been hurt — and he'd hurt others. And now, he wanted fun. He didn't want to give May a piece of himself. Ben was exhausted by dating. He'd fucked up badly. And that's what he would always be when it came to women, a fuck up.

May walked into the bathroom and stripped off his shirt. Her rich ochre colored body was hypnotizing. She turned on the water and stuck her hand underneath until it ran hot. Ben couldn't take his eyes off her breasts or her perfect ass. He stripped down to nothing, enjoying the way she cast a glance at his flawless six-pack and thick built musculature.

"I think it's hot enough," May murmured.

Her shyness was adorable.

With his large piece of man meat swinging between his legs, Ben hopped into the shower and May followed behind. His large shower head easily coated both of them with steaming hot water. May felt her muscles relax as the strong water pressure burnt off the sleepiness from her body. While in the shower, she couldn't help but take a close look at Ben's physique.

Ben moved closer to May before she could soap herself down and he kissed her tenderly. There was nothing lusty about the way he kissed her this time. In fact, May had never felt such soft intimacy with Ben before. She pulled away in surprise, but before she could say anything, Ben kissed her that way again. May thought it would be best not to bring it up and to just enjoy the way his lips felt against hers.

After a few kisses, Ben handed her some soap and thankfully, a washcloth. They both lathered up, but instead of washing their own bodies, Ben moved to clean May's body with gentle scrubbing. They washed each other's bodies until they were clean. Each gentle stroke of the washcloth fired up more anticipation for what they were about to do.

When they got out of the shower, Ben handed May a large and fluffy ivory robe. They dried off and wrapped up in their robes. Ben still couldn't keep his eyes off May. He couldn't stop wanting her in bed. He'd promised himself he'd start off slow with her this morning, but since she was asking for it, Ben wanted to deliver a full experience.

He knew that in order to do that, he'd have to prime May and get her nice and wet. In their robes, they retired to his bed. Ben could feel his cock jump to attention as he watched May nestle in between the sheets. His need to dominate her took control.

"Take the robe off," Ben commanded.

"Now?" May wondered.

Ben nodded.

"Yes," He replied, "Now. I want to see your beautiful pussy."

May took her clothes off and exposed her body fully to Ben.

"Mmm," He mumbled, "Perfect."

May felt self-conscious exposed like this, but

she could see the lust in Ben's eyes and she knew that he wanted to make her cum — possibly even harder than he had before.

"Lay back," Ben commanded, "And close your eyes. We'll start slow."

May obliged. She rested her head on Ben's down pillow and closed her eyes.

"Don't open your eyes," He added, "Just allow yourself to feel."

Ben started to plant kisses on May's naked body. He started with her breasts and then moved his lips down to May's waist and her thighs. Ben's lips trailed across May's thighs and came closer and closer to her wetness. May was heaving with anticipation, eager for Ben's lips to go exactly where she wanted them to go.

"Please…" She whimpered.

Ben loved hearing her beg and she knew it. Once he heard the words come out of her mouth, it was instantaneous action. He planted his tongue between May's pussy lips and began to lick at her wetness fast and furious. She let out a loud gasp as Ben pressed her thighs into the bed and began to french kiss her pussy lips like it was nobody's business.

"Yes!" May moaned.

She arched her back and spread her legs wider, giving Ben even greater access to her fleshy folds. Her sensitive pearl had turned into a hardened nub with desire. Ben's tongue then became singularly focused on her clit and he began to lap at her folds more and more.

"Oh yes! Oh yes!" May moaned as she approached her climax.

Pleasure released hard and fast. Ecstasy began to ravage her body as waves of orgasmic pleasure shot through her limbs and kept her trembling beneath Ben's grasp. Despite the juices flowing from her wetness, Ben continued to lap at May's folds. He pushed his tongue deep inside her until she writhed in the throes of another orgasm.

"Ohhh," May cried out again.

Her thighs were soaked. Ben's face was covered in her juices. She gasped for breath as heat emanated from her flesh and powerful sensual energy was exchanged between her and Ben. She could tell how badly Ben wanted her and how much he would have liked her to return the favor. May sat up and pulled away from Ben.

"What's wrong?" He asked.

"It's your turn."

"Really?"

"Yes. I want to feel your big hard cock filling up my mouth," May replied.

She surprised herself with her words. She'd never used dirty talk before but it felt *good*. With Ben, she was starting to feel more confident sexually. Hell, if he could keep all his kinky desires under wraps, maybe it didn't make her a bad person to explore those kinky desires of her own.

May pushed Ben onto his back and positioned herself between his thighs. Ben undid his robe and exposed his half-erect cock for May to see.

"Mm," She started, "It looks delicious."

"I want your pretty mouth to choke on my dick," Ben followed up with.

May began to get to work on Ben's cock. She began to slowly lick the head of his member until he began to get nice and hard. Then, May thrust his cock deep down her throat. Ben groaned.

"Oh yeah… Take it… Take it…"

***

The taste of Ben's hot meaty man flesh filling up May's mouth drove her wild. She couldn't wait for him to pummel her with his cock after all of this was finished. Ben grunted and held her head down onto his cock. He drove her lips up and down his shaft quickly until his dick was covered in spit.

May could feel him getting harder and harder as he came dangerously close to a climax of his own. May began to use her fingers to massage Ben's velvety balls as she took his hardness as deep as she could go. May started to choke and her nostrils were too clogged for her to breath. She felt divine submitting to Ben's desires like this — even choosing to choke on his cock over breathing.

***

She pulled off at just the last moment and she could tell Ben was close to cumming. May wrapped her lips around his cock again and began to bob her head up and down furiously. Ben groaned as she took him deep and then began to bob faster and faster. He grunted and then finally finished. May nearly choked again as his thick spurts of cum filled up her mouth. She clamped her lips down tighter and began to swallow Ben's seed as it erupted from his magnificent staff.

She didn't remove her lips until her throat was chock full of his thick pumps of pearl-white cum. Ben looked at her teary face, a dusky blushed color, and saw the satisfaction in her eyes from a job well done. He couldn't wait for round two.

* * *

Ben got off the bed after he'd cum and he looked at May, sitting there with a look in her eye as if she were wondering about the job she'd done.

"That was incredible, May," Ben said.

May lowered her gaze, "Thank you."

"But now I want to give you something more intense. I think we're ready for a different safe word."

"Like what?"

Ben grinned. He enjoyed May's eager attitude when it came to their sexual exploration. She had started off shy, but he'd slowly managed to open her up over a short period of time. Now, he was ready to share the special safe word he reserved only for women with whom he had an intense connection.

"Mercy."

"Mercy?" May confirmed.

"I want you to beg for mercy if this gets hotter than you can handle."

May doubted that it would. Ben was slipping into his dominant state and May could see the transformation.

"Lay on your back and spread your legs," Ben commanded.

May did as she was told. She lay on her back

butt naked with her legs spread. Ben moved towards his dresser drawer that seemed to contain an assortment of toys. He pulled out two navy silk scarves and then walked back towards where May was lying in bed. He took one of her wrists and fastened it to the bedpost. Then Ben moved to the opposite wrist and fastened May to the bed again.

"Test the binds," He commanded.

May tested them. And as before, she was securely fastened without any pain.

"Good," Ben assured her.

He could feel himself getting hard watching her tied up there — tied up where she couldn't leave or escape.

Bound & Gagged

* * *

He began to climb onto the bed with yet another scarf from his collection. He fastened the scarf around May's eyes. She was blind to her surroundings and unable to move. All she could do was listen to predict Ben's move and then of course, respond to his touch.

Ben positioned himself on the bed with his fully erect cock. He took warm massage oils infused with a pungent eucalyptus scent and squirted a few drops onto May's body. She recoiled from the cool temperature of the oil. As Ben began to oil up her brown skin, May felt her skin tingling and then warming up. There was something in that massage oil that was heightening all her senses and creating fiery surges of ecstasy throughout the surface area of her skin.

* * *

"Mmm," May moaned.

Ben continued to massage her bosom, then her tummy, then her thighs. He dipped his fingers between May's legs, testing how ready she was for entry. She was dripping wet. Ben stuck his fingers that were covered with her juices into his mouth. May tested good with the delectable sweetness of pineapple juice.

He took his hardness and began to press his cock into her slit between her raised legs. May cried out as Ben inserted his cock in one large thrust. May tried to move her arms to grab onto Ben's back and control the pace, but she was stuck succumbing to his pleasure and his desires alone.

Ben began to thrust into May's pussy hard and

fast. She could feel her pussy growing wetter and wetter. The sensory deprivation caused the ecstasy from each thrust to be even more intense than May had experienced before.

She cried out again and again.

"Ohhh!" May moaned.

"You like that huh?" Ben grunted, "You like it rough and nasty? You like taking my big hard dick up your tight little cunt don't you…"

All May could do in response was whimper and moan as Ben began to pound her harder and harder. Then, Ben began to snake his hand over her collar bone and ease it up towards her throat with each ardent thrust. May knew what was coming next and a part of her wanted to beg for mercy before his hands wrapped around her throat and squeezed.

But in the throes of ecstasy, she hungered for Ben's complete domination more than ever before. The last thing she wanted was to put an end to the never ending waves of pleasure emanating from her core. Ben's palm wrapped around May's neck and he squeezed, gently at first so she could still breathe.

May reveled in the feeling of being trapped beneath his dominant grasp and she moaned louder and louder as an orgasm wracked through her body. Her pussy clenched tighter around Ben's cock, encouraging his hands to clamp tighter around her neck.

Now, May's breathing was labored and she felt

Ben thrusting furiously between her legs pounding her for all she was worth.

Unable to even breathe, May's body could only respond to the intense thrusting between her thighs. Ben's thick meaty man meat rubbing up against every hot inch of her pussy drove May wild. She began to writhe beneath him and just when she thought she couldn't take it anymore, she came. As she came, Ben released his grip around her throat. She trembled in pleasure and again, tried to move her hands to his body.

Still, she couldn't touch him and he seemed to enjoy watching her wrestling against her binds. May could feel his cock stiffen inside her and she worried that he would make the irresponsible move and coat her wetness with his seed. A part of her craved it, but this time, logic overrode her lusty primal cravings.

Ben began to pound harder and harder as release became more urgent. He grunted and then pulled his cock out of May's pussy. He grunted again and she felt thick spurts of his cum coat the mound just above her pussy. She lay there heaving until Ben returned with a hot rag to clean up his fluids and to towel beneath her legs.

Her pussy was still hot for more of him, but for now, May was deeply and profoundly satisfied.

Ben undid May's binds. He released her from her attachment to the bed and then allowed her time to breathe and catch her breath. Poor dove, she'd worked hard to please him, even sacrificing air for Ben to pound her pussy to repeated climax. He could sense May was getting close to exhaustion, but he still wasn't done with her for the day.

May's wrists were raw from her attachment to the bed. Still, she felt at ease. Her body had released tension upon tension as Ben had brought her to a powerful climax repeatedly. Now, May could tell he wanted more but they both needed a break.

Ben climbed into bed next to her and kissed her cheek.

"So May... How was it?"

"Amazing."

"I'm an amazing lover, aren't I?"

* * *

May cringed at the ways Ben could still be a bit of a… well, a bit of a dick. Still, he more than made up for it in the bedroom. Not every asshole could say that.

"Yes, you're amazing… and arrogant."

Ben grinned and winked. May rolled her eyes and then he pushed her back, furiously planting kisses all over her lips and cheeks.

"You're something else," May whispered.

"Oh yeah?"

"Yes."

Ben kissed her again. He wanted more from May, but what he didn't want was to experience psychoanalysis at her hands. He wasn't ready for a relationship with her, or with everyone. Sure, when they were making love, he found himself envisioning a real future with her. May was the type of woman who could share life in his mansion. She was the type of woman he could abandon every other girl for.

There was just one problem: she was too perfect. May was poised, brilliant, she had her own career and she rocked his world in bed. Ben knew he would ruin her. Every woman he touched had changed from a sweet, loving being to a vile creature, writhing with rage. Ben didn't have the heart to change May. For now, they'd both have fun, but when things got complicated, Ben knew he'd have to run.

It would be the only way to save her.

* * *

While kissing her, Ben's fingertips traveled all over May's body. He became drunk on the feeling of his rough hands running over her soft, smooth skin.

"Get on all fours," He growled into her ears.

Each request was a test of her obedience. She fulfilled his request. May positioned her body on all fours and kept her legs together closed, making a juicy looking slit out of her pussy. But now, Ben wasn't interested in her pussy. He was mesmerized by her perfect tight asshole and what he really craved more than anything was an opportunity to dive between her perky cheeks and slide his cock into that forbidden entrance. He'd have to really take things slow. May didn't look like the type of girl that had taken it up the ass.

Ben retrieved his massage oil and dripped some onto May's ass and pussy. He could tell that she was still ignorant to what was coming next. That made him even more excited to plunge between her perfect cheeks.

Ben massaged her ass beneath his steady palms and he allowed his fingers to slip between May's pussy lips, priming her for what was coming next. She seemed to like his fingers probing inside her wet pussy and she even enjoyed the sensation of Ben's fingers grazing her tight little asshole.

Ben began to slide his index finger into May's asshole. He got in just the tip when she squealed, "MERCY! MERCY!"

* * *

Ben pulled away immediately. May turned around furiously with an indignant look on her face.

"What do you think you're doing?"

"Putting my finger in your ass," Ben replied with a shit eating grin on his face.

May pouted, "That isn't funny."

"Why?" Ben replied, "Are you scared?"

"Scared?" May retorted, "It's gross. Plus, I've never had anything up there."

"You've gone your whole life without *anyone* putting anything up your ass?" Ben replied.

* * *

May hated that arrogant look on his face like somehow, she was the strange one for never shoving anything up her butt.

"Yes," May replied, "And I think I've been just fine thank you."

Ben shrugged, "Well, if you want, I can make it feel good."

"How the hell could *that* feel good?" May spat back.

Ben grinned, "So after all this you still don't trust that I can make you feel good?"

May thought about all the orgasms she'd had just this morning. From the moment she'd met

Ben, he'd unlocked more and more about her sexuality. She wanted to put up more of a fight, but with him, she never seemed to actually do it.

"I don't want anything up there. What if it's dirty?"

Ben shrugged, "So what? I knew what I was getting into. And it won't be... It'll be hot."

"And I'll feel pleasure?"

Ben grinned, "Of course you will. Anal orgasms will get you hooked."

May was tempted. She nodded and then said, "OK Fine. You can do it. But *please* be gentle."

She returned to her position on all fours. Ben

felt like he'd won the jackpot and he had every intention of being anything *but* gentle. What he really wanted was to use May's ass like it belonged to him and deposited a load of cum in her forbidden hole.

On all fours, Ben began to work May's ass slowly just as he'd done before. He took his finger and rubbed around her puckered hole. When Ben began to work his first finger in deeply, May began to experience some of the pleasure she was promised. It was a strange, brand new kind of pleasure that felt like it was emanating from even deeper inside her.

She let out a soft moan as Ben plunged his finger even deeper.

"I'm adding a second one," He informer her.

* * *

May whimpered, but she didn't yell out the safe word. She allowed Ben to add a second finger as he probed her ass and began to stir the beginnings of a deep climax from within.

Ben slipped his fingers out of her ass slowly and then added more oil.

"I'm going to put my cock up your big ass," He announced.

May felt her pussy twitch at his words. No matter how logic protested, once she got into bed with Ben, she wanted nothing more than to be owned by him completely. She felt Ben inching his cock closer to her asshole and May tried to breathe deeply to relax and prepare herself for taking Ben's big fat cock.

* * *

Ben began to slide his hardness into May's asshole. She braced herself as she felt his bulging head slip past her sphincter. Ben groaned as he felt May's perfect tight asshole clamping around his cock. Goosebumps prickled over her skin and Ben grabbed her ass as he began to plunge his dick deeper and deeper. May cried out loudly as pain surged through her body accompanied by pleasure.

The pain was immense but May had gone so far that she had no intention of crying out for mercy. She craved the most taboo orgasm that Ben could give her and she'd accept it graciously.

"Harder…" She whimpered, the masochist in her taking over.

***

Ben shoved the rest of his length deep inside May's pussy. She cried out again and then he began to pump his full length into her tight asshole. Just as Ben had promised, May felt her body explode in instant orgasm. It wasn't just Ben's cock, it was the fire that had been igniting within her from their first kiss of the morning.

Ben started to thrust harder and harder. May found herself throwing her ass back to meet his ardent thrusting.

"Yes…"

"Take it baby… Take my big hard cock up your ass. Do you like that? Do you like taking my big cock? I can't wait to cum in your sexy asshole," Ben grunted.

Bound & Gagged

* * *

May exploded again and lost her balance on the bed. Ben shoved her head down into the mattress and began furiously humping her ass. He felt himself driving closer to climax as his dick disappeared inside May's tiny puckered hole. She was writhing beneath him like she was in heat and he could feel himself drawing closer to a finale.

"I love watching you beg for my cum all the way in your perfect little asshole," Ben growled.

May came again and the vibrations from her intense climax caused her asshole to clamp down even tighter around Ben's cock. She whimpered and then felt Ben's cock enlarge and then stiffen inside her butthole. Ben gripped her ass cheeks and let out loud grunts as his hot juicy cum filled up May's hot ass. He smacked her ass as he deposited the last drops of cum in her asshole and then he pulled out, pushing May onto her back.

"Ahh," Ben exclaimed, "That was good."

For May, it had been beyond good. She hadn't expected to find herself in a position where she was so connected to Ben. But with his cock shoved up her ass and with pleasure reverberating throughout her body, May couldn't avoid that deep sense of connection. It was the last place she'd expected to find it — but it was there, a deep sense that Ben was right for her.

Which was why his next words surprised her.

"Come on, let's get you out of here. I don't want

thinks to get confusing. This is just a sex thing, right?"

May felt shame rush to her face. Here she was, thinking that for once they were on the same page about how connected they'd felt. Meanwhile, Ben couldn't wait to ship her out of his bedroom. He'd already wanted to kick her out earlier — it was she who had pushed to stay. That made May feel even more foolish.

"Yeah. Right," She replied, unable to hide the disgust and anger in her voice despite her best efforts.

"Is something wrong?" Ben asked.

May rolled her eyes, "No. Let me just get my clothes on. I don't want you getting the wrong idea. I'm not here to share feelings with you."

Ben watched his spit fire bedmate search his room rampantly for her clothes.

"They're in your bedside drawer," He offered.

May shot him a glare and then muttered, "Thanks."

"Was it something I said?" Ben replied.

May laughed.
"Something you said? Don't play dumb with me Ben. There's no way you're crazy enough not to know what the hell you're doing wrong."

Ben folded his arms. She was right. It was one of the first times a woman had ever stood up to him like that and called him out on his bullshit. It felt... infuriating, but a bit relieving. Ben knew he was the sort of guy who only did as much as he felt like he could get away with. May wasn't going to let him get away with this.

She started dressing and shot back at him, "You know, if you don't want me here, I'll leave. I'm not going to come begging around like some tramp. I'm not that kind of girl."

"So what kind of girl are you?" Ben asked, fully aware that he might be getting himself into hot water that he was unprepared to escape.

May looked at him as she slipped back into the dress which now felt skanky against her skin.

"I'm the kind of girl who doesn't play games

and I won't chase after a man who does. So screw off Ben."

She slipped her heels on and then walked away. Ben couldn't help but bite down on his lower lip as he watched her ass jiggle. She threw open his bedroom doors and continued to walk out without looking back. Ben felt a sharp pang in his chest when he realize that she didn't care if he chased her or not.

"May!" He called, "May wait!"

But there was no turning back. May didn't have it in her to stay where she wasn't wanted.

4 Wedding March

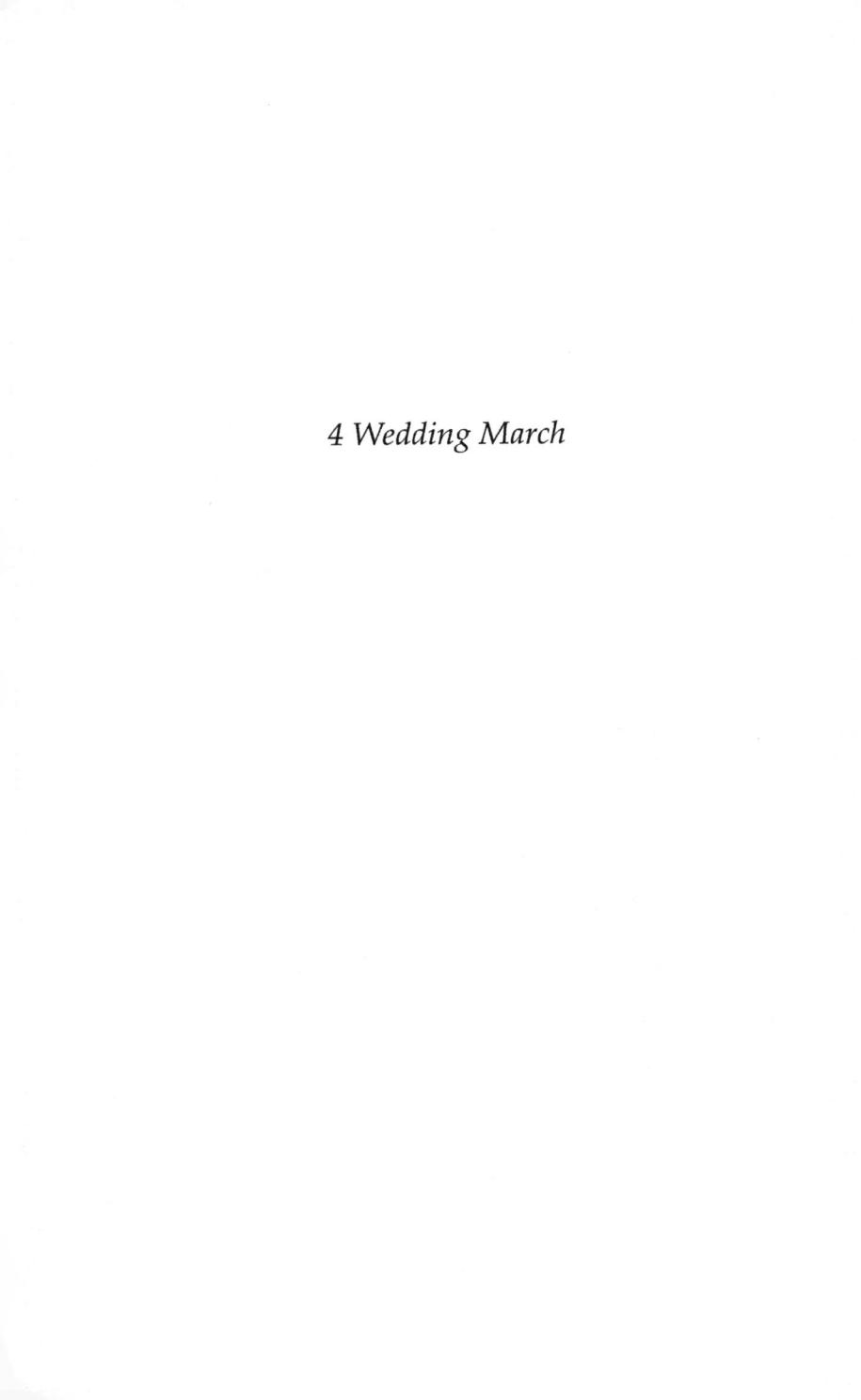

It had been two weeks since May left Ben's mansion. She knew that she couldn't allow herself to meet up with him again. Before, she'd been led astray by dastardly fantasies and incredible sex, but she was finished with recklessness now. Ben was smoking hot, he was charming, but that didn't mean he was worth wasting time on. Hell no. He had to bring something more to the table.

After those two weeks, May hardly had time to think about Ben anymore anyways. Kristin was getting married. For the second time, May met Kristin's fiancé. She cringed in irony at meeting him — his last name was Hawthorne too, like Ben. May wondered if it was some kind of sign. If it was, she wasn't willing to listen.

She hadn't cut Ben off completely. He'd still

send her flirty texts of pictures of his abs after a hot sweaty workout. May returned the favor, but she refused to let things go past flirtation. No more sex. No more dates. No more silk dresses that made her lose her damn mind. May didn't want to ruin Kristin's wedding with her drama either so she told Kristin that things were over with her mysterious new fling. Kristin never even knew his name.

May looked in the mirror of the dressing room and stared at her body in the maid of honor's dress. Kristin had done a good job selecting a royal blue dress that stood out against May's deep ochre colored skin. The dress hugged her curves without revealing too much and May felt comfortable and confident with what she was wearing.

Kristin snapped her out of her reverie by knocking on the door to May's dressing room. When she entered, May gasped.

"Can you please zip me up?" Kristin asked, "I need to let Zahira and Sydney do my makeup."

"Where's your sister?"

Kristin rolled her eyes, "You know Jen. She's late, as usual."

"How much time do you have before you become a Mrs.?"

"Forty minutes."

"Jeez."

Kristin sighed, "Is it weird that I'm nervous?"

"No. I'm pretty sure that's normal."

"Good," Kristin sighed.

Her face then took on a serious tone, "Oh yeah, I forgot to tell you… stay away from the Best Man."

"Who?"

"The best man!" Kristin emphasized, "I know it's tradition or whatever, but Xander's brother is seriously disgusting."

May didn't think that Kristin had anything to worry about. After Ben, she'd practically sworn off men again.

*　*　*

"I don't think you have to worry."

Kristin scoffed, "Oh yeah you do. He's ridiculously charming, but complete scum. Trust me. One of my girls from tennis dated him and he's a total asshole."

"Well trust me, I've had my fill of assholes," May mumbled.

"Good. Thanks girl!"

May zipped up Kristin's dress and watched her bobble off to get her makeup done. She looked beautiful and May couldn't believe that her crazy friend from all those years ago was finally tying the knot. She hoped the guy was worth it.

*　*　*

After doing her own makeup, May followed Kristin to her main dressing room where the rest of the bridesmaids fussed about her makeup. Kristin's sister Jen finally arrived and she offered Kristin a sip of vodka to calm her nerves as she got ready for her final moments before walking down the aisle.

When they were all ready, they lined up in order. The manor that had been rented for the wedding was gorgeous, the perfect setting for Kristin and her 300 guests. May couldn't believe it was all happening so fast — and that was how fast it could happen. Kristin had been one of those girls convinced she would die single but now she was walking down the aisle.

May stood right behind Kristin as they waiting in the wings for the first notes of the wedding march. When the march began, Kristin stepped out. Then the maid of honor and bridesmaids. May was focused on the crowd. The march continued as they walked down the aisle, showered with white rose petals. Some in the audience were crying, but most of them were transfixed by Kristin — the vision in white.

When she got to the altar, May bowed her head and walked to her position next to the groom's wedding party. When she finally lifted her head and looked out towards the audience, the wedding march stopped.

May felt a nudge in her side. She turned her head sharply to see which member of the groom's party had so rudely nudged her. May felt her heart drop to her chest when she saw him — Ben freaking Hawthorne was standing right next to her. And he was the best man.

If May weren't in such an uncomfortable position, she would have screamed. Instead, she held onto her bouquet and stared ahead at the crowd. He wouldn't get a lick of her attention, not now, not ever again. Apparently, Hawthorne wasn't such a common name and the guy she'd been trying desperately to shake was in fact the brother of the groom.

Just my bloody luck. May thought to herself.

"You look sexy," Ben whispered into her ear.

May felt her face turn red, but she just glared at him. Ben smiled, a broad smile that said he didn't give a damn how angry she was with him. This was all another game of cat and mouse to him. And now, May really felt trapped. She had to stand next to Benji throughout this entire wedding and there wasn't a chance in hell he'd leave her in peace throughout the ceremony.

May tried to focus on the pastor who had just started to officiate. Today had to be about Kristin — 100% — there was no time for Ben Hawthorne whatsoever.

The pastor went on and on about true love and the modern era. May could hardly listen to him. She couldn't stop stewing about the fact that of all the Hawthorne's in the world, Ben just had to be related to this one.

"Hey you," Ben whispered in May's ear about halfway through the ceremony.

* * *

She'd ignored all his attempts to get her attention and she was getting sick of him continuing to poke and prod at her.

"What?" May hissed.

"Oh so now I exist?"

May rolled her eyes and went right back to ignoring him. It had been easy to forget how obnoxious Ben could be when they were just exchanging text messages. Now that they were standing next to each other, May couldn't stop feeling prickled by every little thing that Ben did.

"I can't wait to dance with you," He whispered again.

* * *

May ignored him. She wouldn't be dancing with Ben — or going near him. In fact, Kristin had explicitly warned her that Ben was a scumbag. Well, after sleeping with him a few times and experiencing his emotional dishonesty, May had to agree with Kristin. The only issue was she'd already slept with him. And despite the wisdom going on in her head, her heart was still quite foolish.

The pastor finally pronounced, "Yates Alexander Hawthorne, do you take Kristin James Shepherd to be your lawfully wedded wife?"

"I do."

The pastor asked the same question to Kristin, "Do you take Yates Alexander Hawthorne to be your lawfully wedded husband?"

"I do."

They kissed. When they did, May felt her first real pang of envy. She had always dreamed of a wedding like this. Marriage had fallen into Kristin's lap by surprise, but she was still very unfortunately single — and nowhere near marriage.

Ben looked over at May and wondered what was on her mind. He'd watched his brother get married to his preppy little princess and he wondered what his family would say if he were to get married to May. His grandparents would be furious, probably. But Ben didn't care what they thought about him.

* * *

May would be a great wife. Someone else's wife. Ben had promised himself he wouldn't ruin her life but finding himself standing next to her, he was willing to throw away that promise just to kiss her another time. He tried to snake his hands over to hers, but May pulled her hands away. She was growing frustrated, Ben could feel it. And he was defying all his urges to chase after her now that she was pulling away.

Ben wondered how he could be such a screw up while Yates was getting married. How could they be so different from each other? Their parents divorce during their childhood had driven Yates deeper into intimacy with women while Ben found himself utterly terrified of anything beyond a fling.

But May… She was the type of woman he could

imagine cooking up a delicious Sunday dinner. She was the type of woman who he could dance the night away with and share ecstasy in the bedroom with later. She was perfection in brown skin. Ben shifted uncomfortably, feeling his hardness stiffen in his pants. This was the wrong venue for that kind of thing.

Ben tried to force himself to think about the banal — baseball, nursing homes, anything to keep his mind off of May Roberts beautiful soft flesh and her gorgeous plump lips.

The final song of their wedding proceeded and then he followed the bride and groom down the aisle with May. He remembered how she hadn't made it to any of the rehearsals thanks to work. But before then, the maid of honor had been a faceless person, not May Roberts, the woman he desperately wanted. Now, he was being taunted, forced not to give up on her, forced to try again to win her heart.

Outside of the manor, they separated to take photographs. There was no chance for him to interact with May again then. Ben found the photographs boring. His suit was dapper, but he hated being bossed around into a million different poses. Plus he couldn't wait to get to the fun part of weddings — the drinking.

May couldn't stop herself from casting glances at Ben as the wedding photographers posed them all outside the manor. He looked aloof and uninterested. May felt her heart twinge. Of course a playboy like him would be utterly disturbed at the idea of weddings. May felt particularly foolish again for even allowing herself to fantasize about a future with him even for a moment. He wasn't the kind of guy you could build a future with.

The photographs seemed to stretch on for a while, and then they all headed to the reception where there would be wedding cake, drinking and of course, the infamous throwing of the bouquet. May dreaded that charade at weddings. She'd caught the bouquet at the last four weddings she'd gone to but she'd yet to be in a relationship for years.

May had convinced herself that the bouquet tradition was nonsense and she was just really good at catch. This wedding reception had started not much differently than any others. There was delicious food and then there was a toast. May had prepared her toast weeks in advance and after she'd given it, there was enough applause for her to feel a job well done.

Ben didn't give a best man's speech, but his father spoke instead. May saw the man that had produced Ben Hawthorne and caught a glimpse of understanding into Ben's personality. His father seemed humorless, hard-driving and physically imposing; he was the kind of guy who could have you trembling in your boots if he wanted to.

When Kristin and her new husband cut their wedding cake, May felt like crying for the first time since the wedding had started. Kristin looked luminous and not just that, she looked happy. It wasn't just her smile, it was everything about her. She was glowing with joy that May wasn't sure she'd ever experience on her own. And it drove her to tears. At least others out there could find love. That made the world beautiful enough.

Then there was the first dance between Kristin and her father. Her father passed her off to her new husband with tears in his eyes. After watching the couple's first dance, May wished that she'd thought to bring a date to this wedding. She was woefully single on a day where her singleness was painfully obvious. Everyone who came to speak to her asked if she was married and each time, May had to gently let them down.

As she tried to work up the courage to ask Kristin's dorky younger brother to dance, May felt a hand on her shoulder. She knew it was Ben before turning around.

* * *

"Ben," She said flatly.

"May I have this dance?"

It was more of a demand than a question. Ben grabbed her by the hand and pulled May onto the dance floor. She couldn't stop him. He began to spin her around the dance floor in time to the music. May had to step in time in order to keep up with him. Ben held her close, gripping her waist tightly so escape was no option.

"See what you made me do?" Ben said, staring into May's eyes with his impish green ones.

"What was that exactly?" May asked.

He dipped her so low her heart jumped and then brought her back to facing him.

* * *

"I had to go to such great lengths just to get you to talk with me."

He spun May around and as she landed back in his arms, she rolled her eyes.

"You could try not being an asshole."

"Tsk tsk tsk," Ben replied, "Calling me an asshole when you know you'll be in bed with me tonight?"

May felt sick to her stomach. He was so arrogantly convinced that he could change her mind about him, despite his refusal to just be a decent guy.

"I wouldn't get into bed with you if it were the

last thing I ever did," May hissed.

Ben chuckled, "We both know that's a lie. C'mon May. Why can't you loosen up and have a little fun?"

"I don't know. Maybe if you stopped jerking me around I could have fun."

Ben spun her around again twice. When May returned to his arms, he bent his head so it was resting on hers.

"Silly girl… Can't you see that with us, convention doesn't matter?"

"It matters to me."

"Nothing about us makes sense," Ben replied,

"I'm the groom's asshole brother and you're the good girl."

"They warned me about you," May replied.

"I bet they did," Ben answered, "But you know that whatever they said… there's something more here. Can't you feel it?"

"Stop playing games with me Benjamin."

"Whoa. Benjamin. Now I'm in trouble."

"Just leave me alone. Let go of me and leave me alone. I'm not looking for heartbreak tonight Ben."

He dropped her instantly a took a step back. Ben bowed thanking her for the dance.

*　*　*

"Suit yourself. There are more delicious women here I can attend to."

His words cut deep but May knew she had to let him walk away anyways. He was a player through and through. None of his talk about special connections meant a damned thing unless he was willing to put some action behind it. May was too old to be playing these games. And Kristin's wedding was making it painfully obvious that time was running out for her — she'd really be the last of her friends to get married.

May danced with a few more guys. One of them was older than dirt and tried to get a little too hands-on on the dance floor, so May retired to one of the tables and nursed a cocktail of

Fireball whiskey and ginger ale. She let the fiery liquid spill down her throat and searched the reception for Ben. She was starting to regret letting him down so harshly. He was a trouble maker, she knew that, but they still messaged each other often and May had no real reason to be resentful of him.

He'd never promised her anything after all. It was her fault for wanting more.

When May's eyes caught sight of Ben across the room, her heart sank. He'd already moved on for the night it looked like. The woman he was standing next to had a body that had been surgically altered into porn-star proportions. She was wearing a skin tight dress that barely covered her nipples and left all her cleavage hanging out. Ben's hand was gripping her ass.

May felt her stomach turn. The woman's butt was huge. Her waist was perfectly skinny and her laugh was so loud that May could hear it from where she was sitting. Ben was fondling her body and whispering into her ear and the woman was hanging onto him like they were old lovers.

May tried to ignore how hurt she felt, but she couldn't stop her eyes from roving over to the other side of the room where Ben and his new catch were getting closer and closer. May rarely felt envious of other women, but Ben obviously had a special talent for making May go insane. When Ben started dancing with her, May couldn't hide her envy or how pissed off she was. He could really just move on that easily when she'd sworn off dating again because of him.

* * *

May resented how easy it all was for him. All he had to do was to waltz over to some plastic girl and immediately she'd melt into his arms. It wasn't fair. Men had it too easy. May thought that maybe she should leave before she did something stupid. This was still Kristin's night and her stupid feelings about Ben shouldn't be allowed to ruin anything.

5 Coat Check

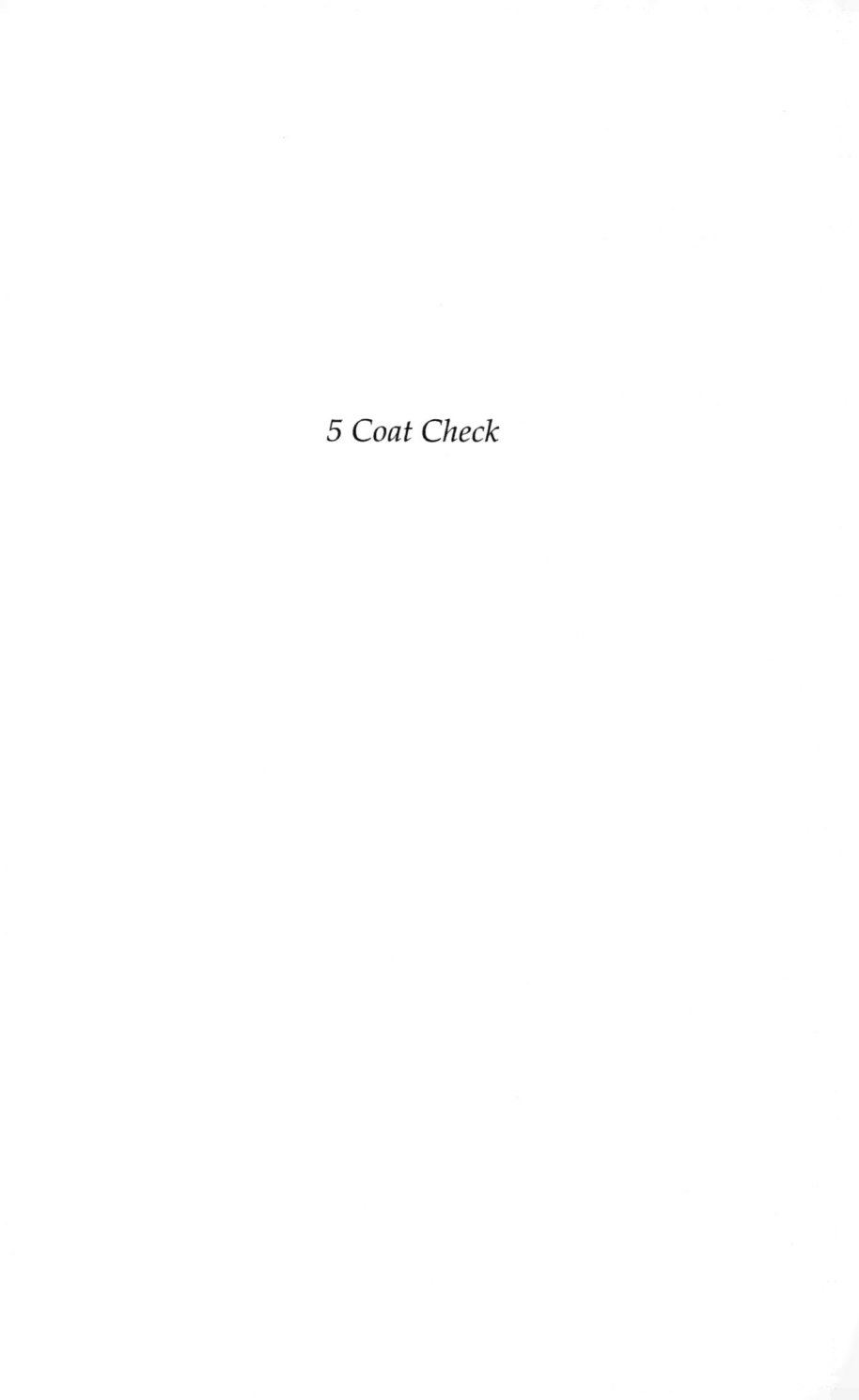

May tried to stick around for as long as she could, but it was hard for her to pretend that she was having a good time. Kristin was happy, but of course, she'd just been married. All eyes were on her and she was having the time of her life with her new hubby. May figured she'd duck out early so she went to tell Kristin that she was headed to coat check to grab her things.

Kristin was nursing a glass of champagne and she was quite tipsy (and exhausted from the long day).

"Hey sweetie, I think I'm going to head out," May said to her.

"Really?" Kristin half slurred, "No!! May we're having so much fun!"

* * *

May smiled, "I know. I think I just need some rest."

"OK. OK I understand," Kristin slurred.

She opened her arms wide and allowed May to embrace her with a nice, big hug. May squeezed her newlywed best friend tightly and then pulled away from her. Kristin waved her off and May at least felt like she had her blessing to leave. Thank goodness. It was tiring watching Ben slobber over some caramel skinned beauty with a perfect manufactured body.

May hated that she cared and she hated that she still had feelings for him. She should have been able to understand that it was just a fling but… everything with Ben was always so intense that it had become all too easy to forget. May started to walk towards coat check, pushing back the tears in her eyes.

Don't cry. Don't cry. Don't be that girl weeping because no one will dance with her at prom again. May tried to keep it together but crocodile tears were streaming down her face by the time she arrived at coat check.

Of course, the attendant was nowhere to be seen and had probably snuck off, thinking that no one would be insane enough to leave a wedding reception as exciting as this one early. May tiptoed and looked over the counter, trying to see if she could spot her coat on the rack. She could see the sensible navy colored pea coat. Summer nights were a disturbingly cold contrast to the sweltering days that threatened to melt her. May tried to find the entrance to coat check when arms engulfed her body in a tight embrace from behind.

May's instincts took control and she dug her elbows hard into the person who had hugged her.

"Ow!!" Ben groaned, "Jesus Christ May!"

He let go of her and May whipped around with fury in her heart and tears in her eyes.

"What on earth are you doing Ben?" She grumbled.

Ben clutched his torso and shrugged, "I'm coming to ask why you're leaving."

May glared at him. Why did he care why she

was leaving? He'd been nestled up with his next catch all night.

"Why the hell do you care?"

"Because I want you May Roberts. I want you badly."

"You don't mean that. You're only saying it because you can't have me. And you're an arrogant bastard who can't take 'no' for an answer."

Ben seemed amused by her response to him.

"You're the one who wanted nothing to do with me, May."

May spoke through grit teeth to stop herself

from screaming at him, "That's because you're playing bloody mind games with me, Ben!"

Ben shrugged, "Don't the mind games make things more fun?"

"No!" May squealed.

Ben swooped in, taking advantage of her flustered state. He wrapped his arms around May and engulfed her in a kiss. He pressed her up against the coat check counter and kissed her long and slow. May pressed her palms against his chest and pulled away.

"Stop it Ben! Stop it right now!"

Ben grinned, "Was that too confusing?"

"Yes!"

Ben leaned in and kissed her again. May closed her eyes and tried to fight her desire for him. But oh Lord, it was too hard. Ben's lips were soft and perfect. He knew exactly how to kiss her. He knew exactly how to make her melt in his arms. May closed her eyes and allowed him to kiss her.

When Ben pulled away, she saw the look of lust in his eyes she recognized from his bedroom. He wanted her *badly* and he'd do anything he had to in order to get it.

"I hate you," May said, looking back into Ben's brilliant green eyes.

She hated him for doing this to her. She hated

him from having so much control over her emotions when her mind was telling her to do the sensible thing and run as fast as she could in the opposite direction.

"You don't hate me May Roberts," Ben replied.

He kissed her again. This time, his hand reached around to her ass and he squeezed her ass cheeks tightly, pulling her close.

"I want to make love to you May Roberts... right... now..." He whispered into her ear.

May felt a twinge of pleasure in her pussy as Ben spoke to her. But really? Right now? They were still at Kristin's wedding. No matter where they escaped to, they could be discovered. This had to be Ben's worst timing yet. Not to mention, May had just watched him flirt up a storm with another woman.

"What about that girl?" May replied.

"What girl?"

"The one you were flirting with."

Ben shrugged, "I was only doing that to make you jealous."

"Bastard."

"Shh," Ben hushed her and then planted his lips against hers again. May's desire for him mounted between her legs and she knew that Ben was right, they had to have each other now.

* * *

"Where are we going to do this?" May whispered.

Ben smirked and then gestured towards the coat check behind them.

"There?!"

"Why not?"

"You're bad…"

"But you like it," He replied.

And yes, May did like it. Ben hopped up onto the counter and made his way to the small door that separated coat check from the guests. He finessed the lock open with ease and pulled May inside.

* * *

"Let's head to the back closet. That way no one will find us."

"What if the attendant comes back?"

"I'll give them a Ben Franklin to keep 'em quiet," Ben replied with a wink.

The walked into the back closet and Ben shut the door behind them.

"Now…" He started, "I want you to hike that dress up and let me see your beautiful ass."

May turned around, facing the wall and then hiked her dress up all the way. Underneath, she wore a tiny royal blue thong that matched the color of her dress. Ben felt himself getting hard just watching the tiny piece of floss struggle between May's voluptuous ass cheeks.

"Oh damn you look good."

"Thanks," May answered.

"I just need to get a taste..." Ben replied.

He bent to his knees and instructed May to spread her legs wide so he could get complete access to the honey pot between her legs. She was wet just being there — standing in a semi public place with a man between her legs ready to get the pleasure of a life time amongst the coats and jackets of all the guests at the wedding. This was beyond hot and the most daring thing May had ever done.

* * *

Ben's tongue darted out of her mouth and licked at the length of her pussy from below. May bit down on her lower lip, trying hard not to cry out as Ben's tongue grazed the most sensitive parts of her pussy. Her clit was especially sensitive and she knew with only a few more licks she'd be mewling in orgasmic pleasure. Ben gripped her thighs and then began to lap at her wetness even more furiously.

May let out a soft moan as she came. Fluids from her pussy poured into Ben's mouth and he continued to lick and lick at May's pussy. When she'd cum another time, Ben knew he was ready for her. He was already rock hard and prepared to thrust his hardness inside her.

Ben stood up and pulled his pants down, reaching for a rubber in his pocket. He released his cock and then rolled the rubber on, spreading

May's legs before lining his hardness up with her tight hole. May braced herself against the wall as Ben began to slide his sheathed cock inside of her tightness.

She breathed heavily as his large dick began to slide into her pussy. Ben was pleased to find that May's wetness was tight and gripped his cock like a vice as he slid inside her. She was trembling with pleasure, too terrified to make a sound in public. He gripped her waist and began to thrust into her hard and fast.

Try as she might, May couldn't keep quiet for much longer. The sensation of Ben's fat cock pounding her hard as well as the sound of him slapping against her thick ass cheeks was driving her wild. May thrust her hips back to meet his thrusting. Pleasure from the taboo exploded through her core and May felt like she couldn't take it anymore.

"Ohhh," She squealed as she came.

Ben gripped her waist tighter and began to thrust his cock deeper and deeper into her. May exploded with another climax and Ben found himself struggling not to empty his load. Ben grunted and thrust into May's wetness a few more times. She moaned and moaned as Ben approached his own climax.

He let out a loud grunt as he emptied himself inside of May. They were both covered in sweat and heaving. Ben stood up, ripped the condom off flinging it into a convenient bin. They stood up in the closet and turn towards each other. May fixed her dress but with the thin layer of sweat on her skin and the disheveled look to her hair, she knew that there was no way for her to hide what she'd been doing with Ben in coat check.

Ben was sweaty too. Even in the dim light of the closet, May could tell that his green eyes were shining with even more desire.

"We need to get out of here," He grunted.

"And go where?"

"I've got a limo for the night. We'll head to my place."

May pulled away from him for a moment, "Wait, Ben, are you sure this is a good idea? I mean… This is just… it's too much isn't it?"

Ben grabbed May's hand in the dark and brought it to his lips. He understood her fears. He understood why the last thing she'd want to do was trust him again. But he wanted her. And maybe if she stuck around long enough, he'd finally work up the courage to tell her what it meant to him.

"Please," Ben whispered, "Let's just get out of here before we get caught."

"You're right."

Ben peered out the door and saw that they were lucky. They fled out of coat check and giggled together as they ran out of the manor onto the lawn.

* * *

"My driver's named Roman. He's tall, olive skinned. See if you spot him."

Holding hands, they walked away from the manor towards the cars, both scanning the lot for Ben's limo driver. May's heart was racing, questioning if she was making a good choice. But she didn't care about whether this was a good choice or not anymore. All she cared about was the intense euphoria she felt spending time with Ben. No other guy had been able to inspire passion in her like that.

That had to mean something.

"I see him!" Ben cried.

He pointed halfway across the lawn.

"I'll race you," May said.

She hiked up her dress as far as it could go without exposing her and she began to run across the long as fast as possible. She could feel Ben chasing behind her and she picked up the pace. Air filled her lungs sharply and she began to laugh and laugh at the scene. Two of them — all grown up but kids at heart — racing towards the limo like naughty teens on prom night.

May lost track of her speed and she saw Ben pull ahead of her. She watched his fine ass touch the limo first and she stopped running as he turned around to face her with a big old smile on his face.

"I can't wait till we get back to my place," He

said.

Roman got into the driver's seat and May fell into Ben's arms again. Out of breath and giggling like crazy, they exchanged a long kiss before entering the back of the limo. The backseat of the limo was spacious and had the fresh scent of new leather. Ben cracked open a bottle of champagne and then poured May a glass.

"I think we oughta toast."

"Toast what?"

"My brother and your best friend getting married. Crazy sons of bitches."

"You don't want to get married?" May asked.

* * *

Ben looked at her with a smile and winked, "I dunno. Maybe if I find the right girl."

May had no clue what that really meant. With Ben, she never seemed able to tell. They clinked glasses and tilted the champagne down their throats. May moved closer to Ben and rested her head on his shoulders. He began to stroke her hair and kiss her forehead. She was so beautiful albeit exhausted from the long day.

Ben lifted her chin so her gaze was tilted towards him.

"Kiss me," He demanded.

She obeyed him and planted her lips against him. She always kissed him in such a gentle way, as if he was made of glass. Her gorgeous brown skin shone in the evening light. Ben kissed her back again and he felt his dick rising in his pants. So much for waiting until they got back to his place.

Ben pressed his remote and they both watched the partition go up in the back seat.

"Ben..." May whispered, "Why did you do that?"

She knew why he'd done it, but she couldn't believe that Ben was really going to try to bang her in the back of a limousine.

"You know why I did it."

"But are you insane!" May whisper-yelled,

"What if Roman hears?"

"If he's a red-blooded man like I am, he'll see my predicament."

"It's too embarrassing…"

"Not if you just let go," Ben replied.

He planted his lips against May's and she knew the discussion was over. No matter how she wanted to protest, she still craved Ben's touch and she still hungered for his thick juicy cock to plunge between her folds. Saying no to him never seemed to work out after she'd let him kiss her.

Ben began to hike May's dress up and she allowed it to happen, allowing his warm and strong palms to travel up her thighs and graze over her mound. Ben hooked his thumbs into the waistband of May's thong and pulled it off. With her pussy exposed in the back of the limo, May felt dangerously naughty.

"Your pussy wants me," Ben whispered.

"Please... Tell me he can't hear you."

Ben grinned, "He can't hear me but he'll be able to hear you scream."

May watched as Ben began to unzip his pants. She watched him pull them off and she ogled his cock hardened in his boxers. He was big and he had a stronger erection than she was used to seeing on him. He slipped his boxers down just beneath his ass cheeks and then positioned himself between May's legs.

"Don't worry… I won't cum inside you."

May was relieved that he'd at least said that before hand. She grabbed his back and let out a loud moan as Ben slid his fully erect hard cock into her wetness. Taking his full length was a challenge and Ben didn't waste a second. He began to pummel her pussy hard and fast.

May didn't bother try to quiet herself. She began to moan and moan with each thrust — certain that the driver could hear her. Ben clamped his lips down around the flesh on her neck and began to furiously pound her pussy. May cried out in euphoria as she climaxed. Ben grabbed onto her hips, squeezing her flesh as he continued to slide into her hard and deep.

***

"Don't stop… fuck me…" May moaned.

Ben began to move harder and faster. He wanted to finish again before they got home. The twists and turns of the limo faded into the background as he focused solely on May's yelps and mewls of pleasure. He drove his dick harder and harder into her pussy and focused on bringing her to yet another orgasm.

May came again and as she screamed and writhed beneath him, Ben pulled out his cock and squirted his cum onto May's face. Moaning in pleasure and with Ben's cum covering her face, May felt hotter than she ever had in her life. Her pussy was soaking wet and burning up with pleasure. She loved the naughty feeling of Ben's cum covering her face and as she gasped for breath, she could sense they were arriving at Ben's place soon.

They sat up and Ben cleaned her off, toweling off her face with the bar towel.

"Sorry if I fudged your makeup," He apologized.

May didn't mind. For the orgasm she'd had in the backseat of the limo, it was well worth it. By the time they arrived at Ben's, they were put together enough to disguise the fact that they's had kinky sex in the back of the limo (except for the fact that Roman had heard the whole thing).

When they arrived at Ben's, Roman didn't make a big deal of anything, but May noticed he was avoiding eye contact. Oops. Ben tipped him and then waved him off for the night. Here she was again, in the place she'd never thought she'd visit. May sighed and followed Ben to the door.

No matter how she tried, she could never say no to him. Not on the first day they'd met and certainly not now.

They didn't sleep together again that night, they just curled up in each other's arms until morning.

Except when May woke up, she was alone. Again, she'd woken up in Ben's bed to find that he wasn't there. Like clockwork, a few minutes after she woke up, Annie knocked on the door and asked to come in.

"Mr. Hawthorne has a car for you out front and

I've made breakfast to go."

The message was clear. Again, Ben had used her and was tossing her out with a few pleasantries to try to make the whole thing less uncomfortable. Mission not accomplished. But May got dressed proudly in last night's clothes and she thanked Annie for breakfast before marching out towards the car. Ben had hired a black town car to take her home. The driver was a fat older white woman whose hair was twisted in a bun so tight it had clearly ripped out more than a few hairs of her hairline. But the woman was polite enough and seemed to have no problem driving May right to her doorstop.

She thanked the woman kindly; said woman refused a tip. May was home, alone and more than confused about everything that had happened the night before. She'd been in bliss with Ben. Each time she kissed him, she was sure that the two of them were sharing something incredible. But again, he'd abandoned her without so much as a word of what was going on between them. May felt like an idiot.

She had to be an idiot. Hell, if any one of her friends were in this position, she'd judge them too. Once inside her house, May slipped out of her bridesmaid's dress and into the shower. She remembered showering with Ben and the way he looked at her body like she was a treasure. May felt sick to her stomach. She cleaned up nicely and then got dressed in a pair of curve-hugging dark wash jeans and a plain white t-shirt. May threw her hair up into a messy bun and decided to enjoy the rest of her weekend —

Ben or no Ben.

Soon, Kristin would be at her luxury condo in Hilton Head for her honeymoon. May figured that she could give Kristin a call. Before fixing to call Kristin, May's phone rang. Speak of the devil and he shall appear. Kristin's voice came through clear as a bell.

"Good morning May!"

She was exactly as chipper as you'd expect a married woman to be on the night of her wedding night.

"Good morning," May grumbled.

She couldn't help it. Her night had been pleasant enough but the morning after had soured her mood.

"How are you?" Kristin asked.

"Mediocre. How about you Mrs. Hawthorne."

"Oh stop!" Kristin replied, "It still feels weird."

"Well you'd better get used to it."

"I know," Kristin replied, "Look… May… This may sound awkward but I have to know. Did you stay away from Xander's brother?"

May let out a loud sigh. No, she hadn't stayed away from Ben. She'd been involved with him long before Kristin had given her the warning she'd required.

* * *

"Uhhh," May started. She knew she was an awful liar and just her pause allowed Kristin to see right through her.

"I can't believe you!" Kristin squealed, "You really went directly after Ben Hawthorne…"

May sighed, "Kristin, don't be mad. I can explain."

Kristin scoffed, "Explain what? How could you be such a…"

"How could I be such a what?"

Kristin clicked her teeth again, "Just last week some guy broke your heart but here you are jumping into bed with my husband's brother. It's like you're turning into some kind of skank."

"Excuse me?!" May yelled.

She couldn't help herself. Who did Kristin think she was to talk to her like that?

"Listen," Kristin replied, "I know it sounds kind of harsh but you just can't expect to ever get married if you keep hopping into bed with random guys especially after I told you he was bad news."

"Well I'm sorry I can't be perfect!" May called back, "You know, not all of us have hundreds of guys lining up! I get lonely too Kristin! And it's not my fault that men play me like a fiddle."

Kristin sighed, "Well May, maybe they

wouldn't play you if you stopped jumping into bed with them."

Her dry tone made May's blood curl in anger. How dare Kristin judge her after all they'd been through. She'd held Kristin's hair back after many nights at the club that ended in too many wine spritzers thrown up into a club bathroom. Now that Kristin was married, she was already different. She already thought she had all the answers to everything in life. It wasn't fair.

May sucked her teeth, "I can't believe this is how you're talking to me Kristin."

Kristin sighed, "Listen, I know we both hate fighting but I'm serious May. You can't keep letting guys like Ben into your life. It won't end well."

* * *

"And I guess you're the expert."

"May… I'm married," Kristin said.

May hated her patronizing tone. So much for getting support from Kristin over Ben's confusing ways.

"You know what. Let's not do this right now. Enjoy your honeymoon."

She hung up without waiting for Kristin to respond. May slammed her phone down on her countertops and let out a squeal. Kristin could get so irritating and patronizing when she thought she was right. May hated opening herself up for judgment. Kristin did have a point about her not heeding her warning, but she still hadn't listened long enough to find out that "the guy from last week" and Ben were the same person.

Her warning had always been too late.

May picked up her phone and tried to call Benjamin again. The way he'd left her that morning had infuriated her but maybe she'd jumped to conclusions. If she was wrong and Ben had a reasonable explanation for everything, that would prove Kristin wrong. At least then May wouldn't feel like such a damned fool…

Of course, Ben didn't pick up. May shut her phone off and lounged back on her couch, thinking shamefully about how easy she'd made it for Ben to use her. May couldn't help caring about him. No matter how hard she wanted to tell herself to forget about him or to dismiss Ben as an asshole, she couldn't help but think that he'd just never been loved properly. He just didn't know how to treat a woman without being an asshole. Could she really fault him for that?

Those moments when he did let his guard down, he was the romantic who would arrange a fireworks show for a date or rescue a damsel from the distress of an incompatible date. He was scared — and May was too — but May hoped that he'd change. If he couldn't — if he'd just hide behind his suave exterior, May knew she had to be final about this.

I hate being so indecisive. May mumbled to herself.

But even the most indecisive woman comes to a

point where she must make a choice about a man in her life. Will he stay, or will he join the others who couldn't rise to the task of loving a strong black woman? May didn't have much faith that Ben would yet change. Which meant that saying goodbye to him was likely coming soon. At some point, she'd have to decide when she'd had enough and beg her own heart for mercy.

Evening fell and May still hadn't heard from Ben. She'd started preparing dinner for herself and stuck to a simple salad with grilled chicken. May didn't bother fussing when she had no one to cook for. Somehow, it just made her feel more lonely. She flicked on re-runs of a reality TV show she didn't recognize and plopped down in front of the television with her simple dinner.

* * *

May's yoga pants nestled close to her skin and sent sensations of warmth through her body. She pulled the zipper on her hoodie up higher over her bosom and then snuggled into her large comfortable couch.

May had become hooked on the show on tv; when she heard the sound of a car in the driveway she was startled from her near hypnotic focus on the drivel she'd chosen to watch. In the middle of a cat fight between two Californian blondes, May heard a car door open. So it wasn't for the neighbors — it was someone visiting her.

May didn't have to get up to know who it was. Ben was the only person in her life with the audacity to drop by at a moment's notice unannounced. He seemed to think that his presence was always a gift and there was no way that May could have anything more pressing. May amazed herself with how quickly the man she had feelings for could drive her to anger. After the past morning, May's patience with Ben had evaporated. Now that he was interrupting her night of lonely wallowing, she felt even more bitter and resentful.

She walked up to the door and opened it before he could knock or ring the doorbell.

"What do you want Ben," May snapped.

"Whoa. Claws are out."

May's facial expression didn't change.

* * *

"I asked you 'What do you want?',"May replied.

Ben grinned, "What does it look like. I want to come inside."

May snorted, "Uh uh. Not tonight Ben."

He took a step up and placed his foot between the door and the frame.

"Are you serious May?"

"Like a heart attack."

May glared at Ben, expecting him to back off. But of course, he stood right there, preventing her from closing the door in his face and walking off for the night.

"What's with all the animosity?"

May scoffed, "Don't play dumb with me."

"This morning?"

Ben's had lost his broad grin but there was still a hint of a smirk making its way across his face.

"Yes. This morning."

"May, I can explain."

"Save it."

"Please," Ben begged, edging his way into May's house, "Please just give me one chance to explain."

Even May had to admit that the look in his green eyes was genuine. He might have been an asshole a lot of the time, but tonight she was getting sweet Ben. May knew she couldn't allow herself to be swayed by his magical words this time. But she'd listen.

She backed off and allowed Ben into her house.

"Fine. Explain yourself. But that does not mean I have to listen."

"I understand."

They walked into the living room and May flicked her TV off as she sat back down.

"So. What do you have to tell me Ben."

* * *

Ben sat down and rubbed his palms on his thighs.

"You're different May. You're different from any woman I've ever been with."

"And how's that working out for me?"

Ben ignored her snark. May kept staring at him, waiting for some explanation for why he treated her so poorly while claiming she was so different.

"I left this morning because I needed time away from you to think. I needed to think about what I wanted. I'm sorry I wasn't up front. It's never been a talent of mine."

"That's a shame."

Ben lowered his head, "Listen, I understand if you want nothing to do with me… But May, I think I want to be with you."

May felt a lump in her throat as she heard the words she'd been waiting weeks to hear. Or at least they were the words May thought she wanted to hear. This time, she didn't feel the skip in her chest like before and she didn't feel the same kind of desire for Ben. She was still attracted to him, but May had finally realized that he really was more trouble than he was worth. He was a tall, handsome, incredibly sexy bit of trouble.

It was May's turn to speak from her heart.

"Ben, I'm sorry but... I think it's too late."

May stood up and walked towards her front door, "I'm sorry Ben, but I think you should go."

He began to walk up to the door but he didn't reach for the handle. Instead, he turned towards May and looked her in the eyes, hoping that her heart would betray some remaining softness for him.

"Don't do this May. I know I've been an asshole but I'm ready. I'm ready to leave it all behind for you."

"How can I be sure Ben?" May replied, "You play these games whenever you don't get what you want. It's hard for me to take you seriously."

"At least let me kiss you one last time," Ben replied.

May looked up into his eyes and felt a pang in her chest as her gaze fell upon his full pink lips. One last kiss couldn't hurt. May nodded. Ben rushed to grasp her waist and his lips planted against hers. May parted her lips slightly allowing Ben's tongue to push past as he held her in a long, deep french kiss.

May pulled away from him and placed her hand on his chest.

"Ben... Let's just do this one last time."

"Are you serious?"

* * *

May nodded, "But then this is it. Don't call. Don't come around anymore. I'm serious."

Ben nodded, "Alright then."

He bent his lips to May's neck and sucked on it hard. May let out a soft moan as his hands roved over her body. She could feel her pussy craving more from Ben, but she wanted to take things as slow as possible. This was the last time they'd be together — for real this time. May wanted a proper goodbye.

Ben reached behind her and gripped her ass cheeks tightly. May squealed and continued to kiss him back. Ben hoisted May off the ground and she wrapped her legs around him. He enjoyed the feeling of her ass cheeks filling his palms and the soft fabric of her yoga pants against his hands. Ben carried May over to her kitchen counter and set her down.

She kept her legs wrapped around his torso and pulled him in for another deep kiss. With each kiss, Ben realized how badly he'd messed up. This was goodbye. He could feel she was serious — too serious to get taken in with one of his other mind games. His chest was heavy. But it wasn't over until this was over. And Ben needed to give her one hell of a goodbye.

May began to undo the buttons on Ben's shirt and he unzipped her hoodie all the way down, exposing May's bra beneath it. May ran her nails gently down Ben's chest until she got to the top of his pants. May reached for Ben's belt buckle and started to undo his pants as his hands fumbled to slip her yoga pants off her body. May got Ben's pants down first and she saw his massive hardness already bulging outwards, desperate to be free from his boxers. May wriggled enough so that Ben could strip her pants off.

"You look so hot," Ben whispered into her ears.

May said nothing in response. She began to kiss him all over until Ben slid his boxers down over his ass. May gasped when she saw how large and hard his cock was. Saying goodbye to that thing would be a whole layer of mourning on its own. Ben had a truly beautiful dick and oh goodness, he knew how to use it.

"Rubber," May reminded him.

* * *

Ben nodded and struggled to find a rubber in one of his pants pockets. He found the XL rubber and May watched with eager anticipation as he slid the rubber over his cock.

Ben moved closer towards May and she slid her panties to the side, allowing him quick access to the slit between her legs. May gripped the countertop tightly as Ben moved even closer, pointing his hardness at her entrance. She let out a loud gasp as he slipped his full length into her in one swift motion.

"Give it to me hard…" She whispered into his ear.

Egged on by her breathy moans, Ben began to pound May's wetness harder and harder. May cried out as Ben grabbed onto her back and thrust into her like his life depending on it. Within a few minutes he'd worked up a sweat and the room was filled with his intensely sexy musk. May threw her head back in pleasure and moaned spectacularly.

She came as she cried out. A massive climax reverberated through her body and May convulsed in Ben's arms. Ben could feel his cum ready to explode in his balls. He began to ram his cock into May's wetness over and over again. She screamed as another climax ravaged her body.

"Ben... Yes..."

Ben could feel himself getting close. He grunted and began thrusting even harder. May let out a loud moan again and he found himself unable to hold back any longer. Ben let out another loud groan as he came. May could feel his hardness twitching inside her as he emptied his balls of every last drop of cum.

They both shuddered and then separated. As they came down from their orgasmic high, it seemed to hit both of them that this was finally over. They both got dressed in silence. May led Ben to the door, finding it hard to look him in the eye.

"I'm sorry May. I'm sorry I couldn't figure shit out in time."

May didn't respond. She couldn't. This just had to be it. No more Ben Hawthorne, and no more drama. She was sure she'd have feelings for another man — a better man — in the future.

Ben was never meant to be. He was too wild. Too untamed. Too much of a wild card for her to really handle.

6 Gagged

After Ben, May had to prove to herself that she could get over him. She waited two weeks. For the first time, Ben actually listened to her instructions. He didn't call. He didn't text. He didn't do a damn thing to confuse things between them. It finally settled into May's mind that this was over. She couldn't go back and change things now.

The night of love-making in the kitchen had been stuck in May's mind since that night. Still, she knew she'd never move on unless she tried dating again. May had gone on two dates. One of them was with an old college acquaintance who had come into town. The date had gone even worse than her date with Khalil and May promptly blocked his number afterwards. The second date was with a nice, chubby guy in middle management at May's firm. He had been nice enough, except for the fact that his "divorce" hadn't actually gone through yet. Meaning, he was a cheater.

Of course, May couldn't see either of them again and she was getting exhausted by the same old dating drama. It could feel repetitive and with no end in sight, dating was starting to make May unhappy. It was so much easier and more satisfying to focus on her job, to focus on her friends and to just put men out of her mind.

A month since the last time she'd heard from Ben, May had plenty of time to make up with Kristin. Kristin had apologized and she'd finally listened to May's story from start to finish. She didn't blame May for a thing and May was glad that they were back on speaking terms. When Kristin called to invite May to a housewarming party, she was skeptical.

"Pleaseeeee," Kristin begged, "We just bought the new house and it wouldn't feel the same if you weren't there."

May sighed, "Well is Ben going to be there?"

After all, Kristin was married to his brother. May could tell from Kristin's silence that Ben probably was going to be there.
Kristin offered weakly, "Well if he comes you don't have to talk to him."

May scoffed, "Come on Kristin, you know that's bullshit."

"I tried to tell Zander not to invite him," Kristin grumbled.

* * *

"Ah I see, a marital spat already?"

Kristin sighed, "I'm sorry May but after how he hurt you? I don't care if he's Zander's brother. He's a dick."

"I didn't mean to cause any trouble for you guys."

"Listen!" Kristin replied, "It's not your fault. Plus I owe it to you. I was such a bitch before."

"We're already past that girl."

"I know but I still feel terrible."

"Well don't," May reassured her.

* * *

"It just wouldn't feel the same without you. Ben shouldn't be able to ruin that."

May realized that Kristin had a point. No matter how pissed off she was at Ben, no matter how sad and alone she felt, she couldn't let him ruin her friendship.

"Maybe I'll come. I can't let him get between us now, can I."

"Oh thank goodness," Kristin breathed a sigh of relief.

May replied, "So I'll see you in a couple days?"

"Yes!" Kristin replied, "And I'm sure Ben's going to show up all sad that he lost a good girl like you. We can laugh about it over mimosas."

"Oh hush," May replied, though she appreciated Kristin's attempts to make her feel better.

They got off their phone call together after that. The days until Kristin's housewarming passed quickly with the usual levels of mundanity. When the day arrived, May had already picked out her outfit. Kristin and her husband had bought a $1 million dollar brown stone just outside that city and they were headed into a world of preppy perfection. May had her white denim, leather riding boots, grey cashmere sweater and pearls for the occasion.

Before getting dressed, May called her family members. Her mood was instantly boosted by the room full of Roberts' talking to her on speaker phone. When she got dressed, she felt more confident than ever. She could look Ben in the eye and she was sure that she'd feel nothing. If he even came. Kristin still wasn't sure that he would.

May wasn't sure whether or not she wanted him to come. Maybe if she saw him again after some time apart, she'd feel differently. Or preferably, she'd feel nothing. Feeling anything for Ben had proved to be more of a headache than it was worth.
When May pulled her car up to Kristin's driveway, she didn't notice Ben's car parked amongst all the other Mercedes and BMWs. Thank goodness. May arrived at the front door and knocked. When Kristin saw her, her eyes widened.

"May! You're here!"

*　*　*

Before May could reply, Kristin grabbed onto her arm with the force of an Olympic rugby player and pulled her to the side into the kitchen, far away from the room where the guests were gathered.

"What's going on?" May asked.

Kristin smiled her big bright smile that told May something was very wrong.

"Bad news."

"What?" May asked, releasing herself from Kristin's death grip.

"Promise you won't be mad."

*　*　*

"I won't be mad."

"Ben's here."

May's nose wrinkled, "How? His car isn't out front."

Kristin grimaced, "Oh yes it is. He bought a new car. It's the red Mercedes."

"Oh shit… Of course he did," May replied, rolling her eyes.

Kristin was still grimacing.

"That's not all."

"What is it?"

"He came with someone else... He brought a date."

"A date?"

"I'm so sorry..." Kristin said, taking on a pitying tone.

May tried to hide the fact that her heart was fluttering anxiously in her chest.

"It's no problem girl. I don't really care. We broke up, remember? He's entitled to do what he wants."

Kristin didn't seem to buy it. May knew that she hadn't been convincing, but she had to at least try to convince herself. She had tried to let go of Ben and all the nonsense that inevitably accompanied her feelings for him.

Of course, Kristin's husband was totally oblivious to what had been going on. When Kristin and May returned to the main room, he greeted May with a booming voice and then wrapped her in a hug.

"Have you met my brother, Ben? He's one of those successful wunderkind types," Zander said in a mocking tone.

May detected the sibling rivalry in his voice. She suspected that Ben had a complex about it.

"We've met," Ben said flatly.

He clutched the waist of the tall, coke-bottle figured woman he'd brought with him and waved at May curtly.

"May works in finance," Zander continued, "And she's known Kristin for like a decade."

"Wow. That is like... so... like... crazy..." The woman on Ben's arm said.

She seemed sweet, albeit basic. May felt bad for hating her. It wasn't her fault that Ben was involved in an obvious ploy to make her feel jealous.

Ben scoffed, "It's not that crazy. Anyone who's failed business school can get a job in finance."

May glared at Ben and got ready to say something in retaliation when she felt Kristin grab onto her arm.

* * *

"Why don't May and I get some champagne and mingle. We'll see you in a few!"

Kristin tugged on May's arm and pulled her back towards the kitchen.

"I'm sorry," May said once they were out of ear shot.

Kristin sighed, "You can't let him get to you like that."

"It's easier said than done. Where on earth did he find that woman?"

Kristin shrugged and then giggled, "The store where they make plastic surgery barbies."

* * *

May tried to hold back a laugh, "Kristin! You're bad. And it's not her fault Ben is the way he is."

"You're right," Kristin replied, "But are you really okay?"

"Not gonna lie, it hurts more than I thought it would."

"Well everyone has their bad breakups," Kristin tried to comfort her. May wasn't sure she was ready to hear it.

"I just wish it didn't have to be like this."

Kristin wrapped her arm around May's shoulder, "It doesn't. Just try your best to ignore him, okay?"

* * *

They poured glasses of champagne and mingled around with the other guests for a while. Some of them were people they both knew from college; others were no friends Kristin had made at work. Then there were some of the Hawthorne's — not Ben's parents — but cousins and second cousins that Zander had invited. None of them seemed to keen on the topic of Ben.

His reputation as a playboy who could never settle had managed to permeate even a family's unconditional love. They all seemed skeptical that he'd settle with this "new bargain bin find". Ouch. The Hawthorne's weren't altogether nice. They seemed to love Kristin and who wouldn't. She was an all-American dream and fit right into this posh, white setting.

* * *

May wasn't sure she ever could.

They returned to the room where Ben and Zander were locked in furious debate. Ben's date was sitting on the couch with her cellphone out taking pictures of her cleavage. It didn't seem to bother her that Kristin and May had entered right behind her.

She turned around with the phone and flashed one of the photos towards them, "Do you think I look hot enough to put this on Tinder?"

"On what?" May asked.

"It's a dating app," Kristin filled her in, "And sure, you look great."

Kristin's grimace told May that Kristin certainly

did *not* approve. Zander and Ben were growing more and more heated until Ben finally exploded.

"Christ, Zander! It's basic bloody economics! Why can't you get that through your thick skull?!"

The room fell silent after his explosion and Kristin folded her arms like a mother of toddlers who had just gotten into a fight.

"Can you boys stop that? We have guests."

"Sorry…" Ben murmured.

Zander smiled smugly and then turned his attention towards May again.

"So May, why no date? Kristin mentioned you

were dating someone but I can't remember who she was talking about for the life of me…"

Ben looked away and May looked up at his brother trying to hide the hot shame in her cheeks.

"Let's just say it didn't work out."

Zander smiled awkwardly, "Shucks. Well maybe it will work out with the next guy."

Ben scoffed, "Well I don't think that's likely."

This time, May couldn't hold back. She turned to him with nostrils flared and fury in her deep obsidian eyes.

"Why are you such an asshole Ben!? Fuck you!

Fuck off!"

May turned around and stormed off. After her yelling, the chatter in the next few rooms subsided as they listened to see when the next firecracker would explode. But May was finished with Ben. She should have never agreed to come. Her face was red hot with anger — not shame. She didn't regret telling Ben off. He thought he could treat her however he wanted but she wouldn't let him get away with this tonight.

May threw on her coat and started to put on her shoes. Kristin followed after her and tried to stop her.

"May, May are you alright? Don't worry about him. I'll tell Zander to ask him to leave."

* * *

May turned to Kristin, trying to push back the tears in her eyes.

"No, I'll leave. I'm the one who's making a scene at your housewarming. The place is lovely but... I'll have to come over another time."

"I understand," Kristin said.

She hugged May and then reassured her, "Don't worry. I don't think anyone cares that you yelled at Ben. They all probably want to do the same thing."

"Right," May mumbled. She wasn't sure if that was helping her feel better.

She walked out of Kristin's house towards her

car. May got into the driver's seat and plopped her head against the steering wheel. Great. She'd promised that she wouldn't let Ben get to her and then what happened? The very next thing she'd done was let him get to her. May started to cry. She hated this awkward space where she wanted to be over Ben, but she wasn't.

May heard a tapping noise at her window. She turned to look and saw Ben standing there. May shoved the key in her ignition and started the car. He tapped harder now.

"May, open this damn window! Don't drive off!"

May put her handbrake down.

"Please May! I'm begging you! Please don't drive off!"

For once, Ben had humbled himself enough to beg her. For once, she wasn't the one chasing after him looking for something that he didn't want. May pulled her handbrake back up and turned down the car windows.

"What do you want Ben?"

"I'm sorry okay May? I'm really sorry."

May wiped the tears off her face and turned to Ben. Hot red anger fueled her.

"Well I don't care Ben. You were embarrassing me. Now unless you have something else to add, can I go?"

Ben held onto the car door.

"What's really going on here May?" Ben replied, "Do you still want me? Is that the issue?"

"Fuck off Ben!"

"May!" Ben interjected, "Please just be honest with me. If you want, I'll give everything up for you. Michaela and I just met. She doesn't mean anything to me."

May rolled her eyes, "So you really think the solution to this is to break some other girl's heart? Why won't you grow up Ben."

Ben reached into the car and grabbed May's hand.

***

"May wait," Ben replied, "You never told me you didn't want me anymore. So be honest... How do you feel about me?"

May looked at him with tears in her eyes. She didn't owe him anything. She didn't want to tell him a damned thing. But she couldn't lie to him. May couldn't bring herself to deny the fact that underneath all her anger and disgust with Ben, there was still a part of her that couldn't let go of the night they'd first met or all the times they'd made love.

Even that last night in her kitchen was stamped permanently into May's mind.

"Ben... We can't do this. You're seeing someone else."

Bound & Gagged

"So you're just going to drive off?"

May nodded, "Yes. I'm sorry but... We're broken up. And it's for the best."

She rolled her window up and ignored Ben screaming outside it, begging for her to open up the window so he could talk to her one last time. May took off down the street, not bothering to fight back the tears any longer. There were no more last chances for Ben — not until he'd proven to her that he'd changed.

May drove all the way home in tears. There was no song on the radio that could lift her out of her misery. As the latest remixed pop anthem came blaring out of her radio, she just felt worse. When she arrived home, May got out of her clothes and hopped straight into the shower.

She thought about what she was giving up saying good-bye to Ben like this and she wondered if she'd ever stop hurting. May whispered a plea to the heavens for understanding and for her to end up just finding someone who really loved her without any mind games. May was starting to doubt that happiness was in the cards for her. Especially after Ben, she was hesitant to trust the exterior charm and alluring magnetism that some men seemed to possess.

May dried off after her shower and changed into a long pink satin nightie. The carnation pink highlighted May's deep brown legs and as she crawled into bed, she felt another pang of loneliness. Despite being an independent career woman, there was no amount of money or financial success that could replace the warm body of a lover in her bed.

May turned her head towards her pillow and again recalled what it was like to be an awkward teenager convinced she'd never have a boyfriend. Well, May had had boyfriends but none of them had amounted to much. Now her fears had metastasized. This wasn't just about a hot date or popularity. Now each night she spent alone felt like a life sentence to solitude.

Solitude was fine in small portions, but May craved a man's touch. She craved knowing there was someone who had her back. Someone who could celebrate promotions with her or mourn dead pets. She wanted someone to share the big things and the little things. And now, there was no one. The man she had feelings for had taken her on a wild ride. May was convinced that loving someone else after Ben would be the hardest thing she'd ever done.

May tried to rest her head on her pillow, even if it was early in the evening. Her weeping and exhaustion drove her to sleep. May slipped out of her worries into a state of peace. The last thing she thought about was the next day; she prayed tomorrow would bring a different outcome, a new outlook, or another blessing to take her mind off of Ben Hawthorne.

He'd stamped himself on her brain. May's late night plea only served to bring Ben into her dreams. May dreamed that he confessed his love to her. She dreamed that he was surrounded by angels. She dreamed that his face contorted and twisted into a monster's. She dreamed that his hands had turned to claws. And those claws were wrapping around her wrist, dragging her down... down... down...

Plenk!

Plenk!

Plenk!

May sat upright. She was covered in a cold sweat. She'd just had the most horrifying dream and now there was something...

Plenk!

There was something going on in her house. Or nearby.

* * *

Plenk!

May turned on the lamp on her bedside table and then walked to the window of her bedroom.

Plenk!

She approached her reflection in the window and then pressed her face against it.

Plenk!

May stepped back. There were tiny pebbles flying at her window. She approached the closed window again and pressed her forehead up against it. May scanned her yard and then saw Ben. He stood there armed with rocks and waved at her as she made eye contact with him.

* * *

Ben gestured for May to open the window. She reluctantly opened it up and yelled down to him, "Ben, what the hell are you doing here? Do you know what time it is?"

"TWO A.M." Ben yelled.

"Ben sh!! I have neighbors! Get out of here!" May hissed.

"LET ME IN OR I'LL SCREAM DOWN THE WHOLE NEIGHBORHOOD."

"Ben!"

"MAY ROBERTS I NEED YOU! MAYYY ROBERTS!"

* * *

"Fine!" May hissed, "I'm coming to the door just stop hollering!"

May wrapped her robe around her nightie and then head towards her door. Ben was here. May opened her door and saw Ben standing there. May had assumed he was drunk, but Ben was stone cold sober.

"Good evening May."

"What the hell are you doing here Ben? Haven't you caused enough trouble."

"Just let me come inside May and stop playing around."

"Playing around?" Ben chuckled, "Oh May, I'm serious."

*　*　*

"Just come inside and stop making a commotion," May grumbled.

She gestured for Ben to come inside and he did. May shut the door behind her, breathing a sigh of relief that she hadn't had any angry calls from the neighbors or worse, a visit from the police department.

"What the hell are you doing here Ben. It's 2 a.m."

"I have something important to tell you," Ben replied.

His face relaxed into a somber position. He took a step closer towards May and she responded with a step back.

* * *

"Then tell me. Don't waste my time and for the love of God, please don't play any more games with me."

"I can't let you leave me May," Ben replied.

May snorted, "Well I've already left you Ben."

Ben shook his head, "You know that isn't true. You know that you still give a damn about me, no matter how much you want to deny it."

May bit down on her lower lip. She had no counter to Ben.

"I still want to be with you May. I'd do anything."

May folded her arms and rolled her eyes, "And your date from tonight? Where's she."

"Come on May!" Ben huffed, "You know that she doesn't mean anything to me. You know that ever since I've laid eyes on you we've been experiencing something different. Something insane."

"You've treated me like shit Ben. I don't want a damned thing to do with your special connection."

"May," Ben replied, "I'm sorry. Just… please… hear me out."

"You're sorry?"

"Yes."

* * *

May was taken aback. It was a rare moment of humility for Ben. Perhaps a part of him had changed. Perhaps he was coming here for a good reason and not just to play another insane mind game.

"Prove it to me."

Ben stepped closer to May and looked down at her. Their lips were inches away.

"I can prove it to if you let me."

He raised his hand to May's cheek. She shuddered as he drew his hand across her face and ran his fingers over her lips.
"Ben, I can't let you back in this easily."

"Why not?" Ben whispered, bending his head so he was speaking directly into her ears.

May shivered.

"Just close your eyes May, and listen to what your body really wants."

May threw her arms around Ben and let her lips dance close to his without allowing them to touch.

"If I let you kiss me, will I be making another mistake?"

"No," Ben replied. "You won't. I promise you May... Just let me prove how I feel about you."

May nodded, "Please don't disappoint me."

Ben lowered his lips to hers. Chills ran down May's back as Ben's lips touched her own. She shuddered as he pulled her body close to his own and she allowed the euphoria of his lips pressing against hers to wash over her. May closed her eyes and allowed Ben to slip his tongue into her mouth. She pressed back against his tongue and then reached forward.

May could feel Ben's hardness eager to escape from his pants. She rubbed his package, feeling his dick come to life as they made out. Ben pulled away from a moment and held her arms, looking her deep into her eyes. May could tell he was exercising as much restraint as was possible for him.

"Please tell me you really want this," He

whispered.

May nodded, "I want this."

"All of this?" Ben asked.

May nodded, "I think so."

"You remember that word, don't you."

"Mercy," May whispered.

"Good God I've missed making love to you."

Ben leaned forward and kissed May again. She'd missed making love to him too. May closed her eyes and let Ben kiss her fervently. May no longer felt like it was two in the morning. She was wide awake and the fiery passion inside her had revved up to a fever pitch. Her pussy craved nothing more than Ben's hardness thrusting deep inside her. She couldn't wait to pull his hard masculine body closer to hers and run her hands along his toned musculature.

"Upstairs," May muttered, "Let's go upstairs."

She turned away from Ben and he followed her all the way up the stairs. Compared to Ben's bedroom, May's was rather modest. She'd done well enough for herself and she had a queen sized bed and a well designed room. May's room was cozy in comparison to the lavish life Ben lived.

When he stepped into her bedroom, he felt like he'd infiltrated May's secret world. He pulled

May back towards him and dipped her down low as he kissed her. May held onto Ben's torso precariously until he lifted her back onto her two feet and then pulled away.

"Do you have any scarves dear?" Ben asked.

May shook her head.

Ben kissed her again and then pulled away.

"I want you bound and gagged in bed tonight. I'll rock your world May and make you cum until you scream."

"Ben…" May whispered shyly.

"Don't be shy princess. I know you… I know what you like…"

Goosebumps broke out over May's flesh. It was true that Ben knew what she liked. From the moment their lips had first touched he'd become fluent in her body language. He knew how to kiss her and caress her and how to bring her to a screaming, back-breaking climax in only a few minutes.

"No scarves but… I have some stuff in my underwear drawer."

She knew that when Ben said "scarf", he wasn't talking about her nightly head wraps.

"I'm sure I'll find something. Take your clothes off and wait for me in bed."

Ben moved towards May's dresser where he

began searching for items to make their night even more entertaining. Ben found a pair of stockings and then something that looked like a night scarf. May saw Ben holding the silken material she used to wrap her hair. They hadn't had *that* conversation yet at all.

Ben turned towards May and looked at her lying on the bed.

"I found this... durag?" He half-asked.

May tried not to laugh out loud.

"It's for wrapping my hair at night."

"Well... It's going to work perfectly. Get on all fours," Ben commanded.

* * *

May got on all fours before him and arched her back, presenting Ben with a flawless view of her ass and pussy. He licked his lips as he watched her body presented for his pleasure. Ben took May's hands behind her back and he used her scarf to tie her hands together.

Now for the final piece, he had to get May's permission.

"I'm going to gag you now," Ben said.

He knew that if she wanted out, she'd say "Mercy."

"What about the safe word?"

"Trust me... I won't go too far."

May nodded. At least when it came to what went on in the bedroom, she trusted Ben completely. He knew how to have a good time without taking things too far.

"Okay. Do it."

Ben opened May's mouth and stuffed a thong in there. He tied her mouth shut so she couldn't remove the gag.

"Mmmfmfm," May said.

"Good. Looks like it's secure… Now wait… Let me taste you."

Oh goodness. With no way to moan out loud, protest or share her input, May was at Ben's mercy. He could use her body however he wanted to and all she had to do was feel… feel the intensity of his thrusting… feel his ardent desire of her… feel multiple climaxes until she couldn't feel a single thing more.

Ben bent down behind May. Her pussy was slick and juicy wet, ready for him to flick his tongue between her folds. May couldn't move to grab onto the bedsheets or brace herself. She was bent before him with complete vulnerability.

Ben moved her thighs apart the tiniest amount and then he inhaled the fresh scent of May's pussy. As the honeysuckle scent wafted into his nostrils, Ben's desire to taste May grew even stronger.

"Mmm," He moaned.

* * *

He drove his tongue between her folds and started to pleasure her with smooth, long strokes of his tongue. May mumbled into her gags. Pleasure was shooting through her body from her core throughout her limbs. She wanted to cry out but no matter how hard she tried, not a single sound could escape. Ben gripped her thighs and began to stroke at her pussy more furiously.

Ben's wet tongue passed between May's slick folds and she began to thrust her hips backwards as if she were begging him for more.

"Mmmm!" May moaned.

She moaned like this louder and louder. Ben knew he was bringing her close to climax so he kept his tongue working at her folds and used two of his fingers to play with her entrance. May began writhing and trying to moan even more. The gags around her mouth were silencing her and forcing her to just experience the most intense orgasm she'd ever had.

Ben shoved two fingers into May's wetness as she climaxed and that drove her wild. She sent her hips thrusting back on his fingers as his lips continued to work her folds. Ben plunged his fingers into her honeypot and lapped around May's clit until she came again and again.

When Ben was finished, May was a trembling mess. He pulled away from her and then undid her binds. She continued to quiver as he turned her around so she was sitting and facing him.

* * *

"I'm going to remove your gags," He said.

May nodded. The intensity she'd just experienced had been unlike anything she'd experienced before. Ben reached around and undid her gags. May coughed a little bit and tears ran down her eyes.

"Did you enjoy that?" Ben asked.

May nodded. Her legs were still trembling from the ferocity of her climax. She wanted more from Ben. She always did whenever they got started together. But May was still worried about this and what she was doing here. Ben had come back to her and their night was already off to a good start, but she worried. It was hard not to worry with him.

* * *

Ben leaned in and whispered into May's ears, "I'm not finished with you."

She felt a pang of desire between her legs.

"Good," May replied.

Ben planted his lips against hers and pushed her back onto the bed. She spread her legs wide and allowed for Ben to lie between them. He pressed his body up against hers and May ran her hands over his taut, strong muscles. She could feel Ben's muscles tense and relax with each breath. May hungered to feel his cock plunging between her legs.

"Let's take things slow," Ben whispered.

May nodded.

* * *

She doubted they'd show the restraint but it was worth it. Between the two of them, there was so much history, so much that had gone wrong. Despite their feelings for each other they'd both made mistakes and needed to tread carefully. May clutched Ben's back as they made out; she felt his cock pressing into her leg, eager for release. With each breath she could feel her pussy getting slicker with desire. Taking things slow couldn't last very long at this rate…

"I need you… I need you inside me," May whispered.

"Are you sure, May…" Ben whispered back.

"Yes."

* * *

May was sure. This always happened when it came to Ben. She'd convince herself that she was finished with him but her body couldn't get enough of his. You almost couldn't blame her. Ben was tall with gorgeous hair, brilliant luminous green eyes and a chiseled body that was sculpted by the Gods. May arched her back as Ben's lips wrapped around a bit of flesh on her neck. Jolts of ecstasy traveled through her body. Her pussy was begging for him.

"Put it in Ben…"

Ben rolled a condom onto his hardness and then position himself between May's legs. As he looked into her eyes he began to press his cock into her wetness. May gasped and kept eye contact as Ben's thick dick fit inside her wetness. May moaned as he pushed the last few inches in. Ben's dick was still a tight squeeze and she felt his hardness stretching her out. May grabbed onto Ben's back as he began to thrust furiously inside her.

Ben pushed her legs back behind her head and began to pound at May's eager wetness. She moaned beneath him, enjoying the deep strokes that set every inch of her wetness ablaze with ecstasy. May gripped Ben's ass cheeks and pulled him deeper and deeper. She began to feel ecstasy as he plunged into her.

"Ohh!! Yes!! Yes!!" May cried out.

Ben picked up the pace and began thrusting more furiously. He could feel May's pussy tighten around his thick love-snake and his balls tightened as he came close to climax. May moaned as she came around his dick. A thin layer of sweat started to coat them as they panted in euphoria between the sheets.

May's scent filled the room and Ben went crazy with his lust for her. He began to pump into her pussy harder and faster. Ben grunted as May reached another climax. He reached his hand up to her throat and wrapped his hand gently around her throat again. Ben didn't squeeze, he just continued to pump her pussy hard and fast.

May groaned as she climaxed again. Just the feeling of Ben taking control by wrapping his hand around her neck drove her crazy. She wrapped her legs around Ben and began to thrust her hips upwards to meet his urgent thrusts. May could feel Ben getting close and she gasped as she felt his cock stiffen inside her.

* * *

"Cum for me baby," She whimpered, "Cum for me."

Ben couldn't resist her gentle moans. He grunted and then he came. May grasped Ben's body and pulled him closer to her as he finished. His dick twitched one last time between her legs. May caught her breath as Ben gazed into her eyes. She could see his desire had not yet abated.

"That was... incredible," May replied.

Ben grinned, "I know."

He rolled off of May and threw out the condom. He returned to bed. As May watched him return, she couldn't help but bite down on her lower lip.

Damn. Ben looked great. Even better than before. He slipped into bed next to her.

"Mind if I stay the night?" He asked.

May looked over at him in disbelief.

"Only if you're not going to duck out of here in the morning."

Ben looked away for a brief second, embarrassed.

"I won't leave."

"Are you serious Ben? Because I'm not going to get played again."

Ben shook his head earnestly.

Bound & Gagged

* * *

"No. I won't leave you. Not tonight May."

He leaned over and kissed her on the lips. May slid under the covers and faced him. She looked Ben's face up and down, wondering what had changed — if anything. She was still uncertain about him. May didn't know if her uncertainty would change any time soon. It was still difficult to trust Ben. He'd worked his way back into her bed, but May still had her guards up.

Ben rolled over and went to sleep. At first, May pretended to sleep but she couldn't. After all this time, it felt strange to have Ben in her bed again. May sat up and looked over at him. He was breathing slow and deep...

May watched as Ben rolled over onto his side.

* * *

"Iloveyou."

May's heart stopped as she heard Ben's sleepy mumbling. Had he just said what she *thought* he'd said.

"Huh?" May asked out loud.

Ben responded with a sleepy snort and then silence. Great, if she was having trouble sleeping before, it was about to get worse. Ben Hawthorne had just told her that he loved her and May hadn't a single clue how she was supposed to respond. She slinked back underneath the sheets and closed her eyes.

Sleep came easier for May than she'd imagined. With Ben's warm body next to hers it was difficult not to feel secure and safe. May would have given anything in the world to feel safe like this all the time. But with Ben, could she ever really have that? Was he too stuck in his ways to change for longer than a night? As May drifted off to sleep, she half expected him to be gone in the morning.

7 You Love Me?

May woke up wrapped around Ben. He was still there, lying in bed next to her. When May woke up, the first thing she thought about was what Ben had said to her the night before. Ben's confession stuck in her head and May had no idea what to do or if she should approach him about it.

As she sat up in bed, Ben turned around and slowly woke up. May watched as his green eyes fluttered open. He looked around and then sat up.

"Hey beautiful," Ben muttered, with that sexy low sleepy voice.

May leaned over and kissed him, "Good morning."

* * *

Ben turned his legs out of bed and rested his feet on the ground.

"Let me get some breakfast."

"Breakfast already?" May asked, "Why don't you stay in bed and cuddle."

Ben turned around and flashed May a half-smile.

"Naw, I'll get things started in the kitchen. I'm hungry."

"Well maybe I'll come down there, show you where things are and make some coffee."

"If you wish."

* * *

Ben got out of bed and threw on his boxers before starting downstairs. He seemed prickly; May wondered if she was imagining things. Ben just seemed unlike himself. He was getting breakfast but he didn't seem like his usual upbeat self. May ogled Ben's gorgeous back and perfect ass as he wandered downstairs.

She showed him where everything was and then popped some coffee on her coffeemaker. Ben cracked open a few eggs and started whipping together an omelette in a mixing bowl.

"Did you sleep well?" May asked.

The truth was, she wanted to get to the bottom of Ben's sleepy confession. Was he really fast asleep? And even if he was asleep, did he still mean those words?

* * *

"Yes."

Ben's response was flat and toneless. May couldn't make any sense of it. Or him. His lips were pursed and he remained focused on his omelette. There were no snarky comments, no teasing, nothing. He was just quiet. Focused. May had never seem him like this.

As Ben poured his omelette mix into the skillet, May came up behind him and wrapped her arms around Ben's cut waist. She kissed a freckle on his pale back and rested her cheek against him.

"Is everything alright?"

"I already told you that it was."

"You're unusually quiet."

"A man can't be quiet?"

May's coffeemaker beeped. May took a step back from Ben.

"Coffee then?"

"Sure."

"Cream or sugar?"

"Guess," Ben replied with a smirk.

Perhaps he wasn't pissed off after all.

"Black?" May guessed.

* * *

"Yup."

She poured Ben's black coffee and then made her own wit heaping spoonfuls of sugar and a splash of soy milk. Ben took a swig out of his coffee mug and then ran a spatula around the pan to ensure the omelette didn't stick. May took a sip of her coffee and kept her eyes on him.

"You're staring at me."

"Because something's wrong and I can tell," May interjected.

"You're nosy," Ben mumbled.

They drank a few more sips of their coffee. May didn't stop watching Ben. He flipped the omelette over. May studied his face for a hint about how he was feeling but Ben was tight lipped and his facial expression betrayed nothing that was on his mind.

Ben finished cooking their omelettes and served it up.

"Bon appetit."

They sat down at breakfast together. May still thought Ben seemed resistant. His face was screwed up more than before now. He looked visibly unhappy.

"Seriously Ben, nothing's wrong?"

"Damn it May! Can't you just leave me the hell alone."

May looked at him with a raised eyebrow. That was quite an outburst for a man who claimed that he wasn't angry.

"I'm sorry..." Ben grumbled.

"Don't be sorry. I want an explanation."

Ben pushed his omelette away from him.

"Don't worry about it."

"Ben how the hell are we supposed to move forward if we can't even communicate? You need to talk to me."

Ben looked at May's concerned face. She didn't deserve this. He always had the option of being honest with her. But being honest about his feelings had never been Ben's forte. He struggled to bare his heart to anyone, especially to women. He'd done so many women wrong that he knew he'd deserve any mistreatment he got from May. Still, that didn't help things. What would help things was being honest with her and trusting that May wouldn't hurt him.

"Fine. I guess I'm a little on edge."

"I guess."

"Listen, I'm sorry May. I should have never snapped at you like that."

May nodded, "You're right. You shouldn't have. What's gotten into you Ben… Just last night…"

* * *

May trailed off. This was the utterly wrong time to bring up what she'd heard the night before.

"What about last night?" Ben asked.

He wasn't going to let her get away that easily.

"You said... Do you remember what you said?" May asked.

Ben looked into May's eyes. She was close to figuring out what was wrong. Yes, he did remember. Ben remembered how his heart had been pounding as he threw rocks against May's window. He remembered how it felt to finally kiss her again after all that time apart. He remembered how good it felt to touch her soft brown skin and to feel his heart swell with desire and with... love.

* * *

Ben had forced the words out of his guarded heart but May had said nothing in response. Ben had panicked. And in the morning, he was scared to face her. It had taken everything for him to get to this point. But May... Where was she? Did she care for him the same way or was she still testing out the waters.

"Yes. I remember."

Now May was confused. If Ben remembered what he said, why was he behaving like an asshole?

"Ben, last night you said that you... that you loved me."

Ben swallowed and looked away from May. He

was't looking forward to having this conversation.

"I guess I did."

"Then what the hell is going on right now?"

Ben looked at May. His piercing green eyes were filled with anger.

"You didn't say anything."

"Huh?"

"When I told you that I loved you, you didn't say anything," Ben clarified.

It was May's turn to feel embarrassed and exposed. Ben was right. She hadn't said anything in response to him and she didn't even have a good answer as to why she hadn't replied.

"I... I didn't know what to say."

"Bullshit," Ben scoffed.

"Bullshit?"

May could feel her voice rising.

"Yes. It's bullshit May. What else would you say when someone says they love you? There's only one thing to be said."

May looked away from him. She couldn't bear looking Ben in the eyes. Not now. She couldn't bear to be confronted by this. May knew that it would have been easy for her to tell Ben that she felt the same way. But after all that had happened between them, May's heart was too timid for her to confess to Ben that she loved him.

Her reluctance in itself led May to wonder if she really did love him at all or if she'd just been shaken by companionship and mind-blowing sex.

"I don't know if I can tell you what you want to hear," May said.

She averted her eyes from Ben's, expecting an explosion. What happened was much worse. Ben stood up and cleared their plates. He stood over the sink washing up the dishes they'd used for breakfast. May followed Ben from the table and watched him wash up.

He was meticulous about it. He scrubbed each plate like he was getting graded. May couldn't let things hang in the air like this. This wasn't how she wanted things to happen between her and Ben. May was uncertain that she loved him, but she was certain that she didn't want things to end again. It was complicated.

"Ben, please don't do this."

"Do what," He grumbled.

"Don't turn your back on me."

"Well I don't know what the hell you want May," Ben grumbled.

"I want you to listen to me... to give me time."

Ben turned around and dried his hand on one of May's kitchen towels.

"What do you need time for huh? I told you that I loved you May. Isn't that what you want?"

May stood there staring at him for a moment. She took a step forward. Ben took a step forward too. May reached her arms around him and Ben allowed her to. She engulfed him in her arms and ran her hands over his back.

Ben leaned down and kissed May on the lips.

"You drive me crazy, you know that?" Ben said.

May nodded. She could understand that. She

knew that Ben wasn't the kind of guy to settle down easily. She knew that for him, love was a big deal. It was a big deal to her too but not the way it was for Ben. He was slow to open up and once he had, May could tell how scared it made him to admit that. If only she could have time… more time to think about how she felt about him. Or more time to decide if what was happening between them was real.

"Kiss me Ben," May replied.

Ben kissed her. May pulled him closer and thrust her tongue into his mouth. Ben pushed his tongue back and they kissed like this until May couldn't take it any longer. She pulled away from Ben gently.

"Upstairs… Please…"

Ben nodded. He kissed May again and then reached behind her, cupping her ass cheeks. Ben gripped May tightly and then lifted her off the ground.

Ben picked May up and whisked her up the stairs as they kissed and kissed. When they got to her bedroom, he lay her back in her bed where they'd just spent the night. Ben climbed on top of May and she wrapped her arms around his neck. He wanted to tell her again that he loved her. But he would have said anything just to have her say the words back to him.

Ben didn't know if he really understood May after all. He'd tried to do everything to show her that at the end of the night, she was the woman he wanted to go home with. No one else could stir feelings in him the way that she could. He wasn't his suave, cool and collected self with May. He wasn't in control...

For the first time, Ben felt his heart stirring for more than a physical connection. He thought of all the women in his past — like Kim, or Megan. He thought about how all of them wouldn't have believed he could settle down. And until now, Ben hadn't believed it either. But with May, he could really picture a life of more than physical encounters.

Ben pulled away from May and kissed her forehead.

"I think you've cast a spell on me."

They kissed and May rolled over on top of Ben.

Ben gripped her waist as she leaned forward to kiss him. Damn. Ben could feel his dick getting hard as May kissed and kissed him. He was trying to hold back and give her space to decide how she felt but that monster between his legs was starting to wake up. Ben could never resist a good morning romp.

"May…" He said when she pulled away.

"Hm?"

"I want you so badly right now…"

"I want you too."

"Then get naked girl, what are you waiting for?"

Ben was trying to hold onto his mojo. May was

knocking him off his feet and just staying in control of his senses was a struggle. May was driving him mad. Her hands hooked around Ben's boxers and she slid them off of him, exposing his already hard cock.

May squeezed out of her own clothes and then found a condom which she rolled over Ben's hard cock using her lips. Ben groaned as he felt his dick slide down May's throat and grow instantly lubricated from her spit.

"Oh yes babe…" He grunted.

May removed her mouth from Ben's dick and then started to position her pussy above his dick. Ben gripped her hips, holding her steady as she balanced above his hardness. His dick grew thicker as he imagined impaling her pussy on his eager man meat.

May pressed her palms to Ben's chest, the fluttering of his heart sending jolts of pleasure through her fingertips. May started to lower her wetness slowly onto Ben's dick. She gasped as she first felt his engorged head pushing past her entrance. May moaned as Ben's dick started to drive deeper and deeper inside her.

"Take it babe," Ben encouraged her.

"Yes…" May whimpered.

Ben's cock was now fully buried inside her. Every inch of her pussy was trembling with euphoria. She balanced her weight on Ben's chest and began to ride his dick. May rolled her ass cheeks around and around, slamming into Ben's hardness. His dick was digging into her deeper and deeper with each stroke. For once, May could control her climax and she was taking things nice and slow.

May gasped as she felt the first waves of a climax over power her. She moaned and began to ride Ben faster and more furiously. He grabbed her ass cheeks and helped move her up and down his stiffness. May threw her head back and moaned as Ben continued to help her ride him.

Her breasts swung in the air with each bouncing motion and May's hips and ass jiggled with each stroke. Heat built up inside her and exploded again… and again. She never wanted Ben to stop her. Ben's cock was slick with her creamy wetness and May began to gasp and moan again.

* * *

"I'm gonna cum!" May cried out.

Ben grunted, "Now cum for me baby! Cum for me!"

May cried out again as she came. This time, Ben struggled to hold back. He groaned and then released in the thin latex barrier between him and May. May shuddered and then collapsed on top of him. Ben grabbed her hips and pulled her close as she came down from the intense orgasmic high. When May rolled off of him, her smooth brown thighs were coated in a mixture of their juices. Her pussy was still swollen. Ben couldn't wait to get back between her thighs again.

May lay on her back and he rolled over, pushing her hair out of her face and kissing her cheek.

What he felt for her was so damned strong, but Ben worried that he'd already ruined his chances. He'd focused too much on making love to May to actually remember to show her love.

But Ben desperately needed her to love him back. He'd been pursuing May doggedly for so long, he knew he wouldn't take it well if she chose to walk away from him — even if he probably deserved it.

"What's going on in your head, huh?" Ben asked her.

May smiled — a smile that said she had no intention of revealing her hand.

"So many things Ben."

"And what about this?"

Ben felt a lump in his throat as he asked her. He'd never been like this before. For the first time in his life, he was acting like the guy that Kim had wanted him to be. Or Megan. Or any of the other women whose hearts he'd broken. But he just hadn't been able to fake it for any woman. And with May, he didn't need to fake a thing. She'd been the first person to stir a fire up in every part of him. She was the first woman to spur his emotions in the bedroom and out of it.

May shook her head, "I don't know what to think about this Ben."

"I'm here. I'm here now May. What the hell do you need from me to believe that this is real?"

May rested her hand on Ben's shoulder.

"Ben, it's only been one night. It takes longer than a night to prove someone's changed."

"So what then? Can I see you tomorrow?"

May looked away from him.

"So I can't see you tomorrow?"

She shook her head shyly. Ben tried to find the answers on her face, but there were none that he could understand.

"So you want space."
He didn't phrase it like a question.

"I think I need space Ben."

"And what the hell can I do? Just stand by and wait for you?"

May nodded, "Prove to me that you're not an asshole anymore."

Ben sat up. He felt sick to his stomach. She was really prepared to have him leave — even after he'd said that he loved her. But Ben knew he should have expected this from May. She would never be satisfied with words. She needed to see him take action and really prove he was the real deal. Hell, that was part of why he loved her.

Ben started to get dressed. It was strange to be vulnerable with anyone, especially with a woman. Ben hadn't allowed that to happen throughout his dating life. In May Roberts' world, he couldn't get away with being the bad boy or the player. He couldn't get away with not giving a damn anymore.

"When you're ready for me, I'll come back," Ben said.

May watched him get dressed. He was silent as he did so. May didn't know what else to say to him. It would have been nice to tell him that she loved him but May couldn't force herself to trust Ben again so quickly. She had to let him go. As he walked downstairs, May called a weak goodbye after him, knowing that it wasn't enough.

As he left May's place, Ben got into his new car and sped down the highway. He didn't know where he was driving, but he knew he had to drive fast. He stomped on the gas, taking the car to 75 mph. Not fast enough. Ben pressed down harder and took his hot-rod sports car to a smooth 85 mph. There's be cops on his ass in no time if he kept up like this, but Ben couldn't find it in his heart to give a damn. He felt alive. He felt like he was balancing on the edge of life and death in a place where it didn't matter what May thought of him — he was just here, breathing, thinking of absolutely nothing.

The traffic-free driving continued for miles. Ben's hand clutched the steering wheel 'till his knuckles turned white. But when he came upon the next big city, he knew he had to slow things all the way down. There had been no cops, no accidents — he'd been lucky. Ben's heart slowed as his car did and he joined the line of commuters. May Roberts was driving him crazy.

* * *

He should have known she would from the first time he'd met her, tripping all over his table in one of his restaurants. Ben knew it made sense that he'd be drawn to trouble. Hell, he'd practically teased karma for years. And now, May wanted him to prove himself to her and he had no clue how.

All Ben knew was that he had to do something spectacular. He had to make her realize that he was the only guy for her. He had to show her that he wasn't... himself. Ben didn't know how to be anything else when it came to women. He'd always been immensely good looking and as a result, every woman in his life get away with being an asshole. May had said it best: he was an asshole.

* * *

Shit Benji. How are you going to turn things around now?

It felt like Kim was haunting him. And every ex-girlfriend who he'd had since high school. He'd been a dick to all of them, even laughing in some of their faces when they'd confessed their love for him. Now that Ben knew what it was like to really be in love, his gut had twisted up into a million knots. He didn't deserve May. And if he ever wanted to, he'd have to do something difficult.

Ben pulled off his next exit into a town called Homer which was a few miles out of the city. It was another one of America's abandoned factory towns and the place where his first ex-girlfriend from college lived with her husband and two kids. Ben had no intention of going to see her, but being here made him think of the other women he'd hurt.

Ben pulled out his phone and took a deep breath.

I've got to apologize don't I. I need to make things right.

There were so many women he needed to apologize to that Ben knew it would take a while. And then there were the women he'd kept on the back burner — all the women he'd taunted May with while having no interest in them.

May was right — he was an asshole. But for once, Ben was genuine about changing. There would be no other women after May he'd decided. If he couldn't win her back, that was it.

* * *

Do I really have what it takes to be celibate? Ben grumbled.

But he'd always been a guy that went to the extremes. He'd either win or he'd lose. Most times, Ben won. But when it came to May, he was prepared to lose. He knew if he did lose, it would just be karma finally coming back for his ass. Ben didn't bother going to see his ex, but he drove around town for a while and thought about the women he had hurt that he needed to apologize to.

And after that, he'd come back for May in a big way. There'd be not a sliver of doubt in her mind how he really felt about her. Ben was convinced.

* * *

After Ben had left, May felt cold. She hadn't noticed how cold her home had become until Ben was gone. May slipped out of bed into a pair of gingham pajamas and then wrapped her robe around her waist for more security. She needed comforts now more than ever.

May couldn't help but miss Ben once he'd been gone a while. And she hated how she'd left him, even if she knew it was for the best. If he was meant to come back to her, he would. And if he wasn't meant to return, that would be the last of him. Hell, they'd broken up before, May knew she'd just have to get used to it now.

May hadn't spoken to Kristin since the awkward incident at her place. But Kristin called that morning, eager to hear how May's night had gone. May was reluctant to tell her, but asked

Kristin for updates on the rest of the party.

"It was lovely. You know, Zander's parents are so tough on him but I think they really liked the house."

"That's wonderful," May replied, "And I didn't cause too much of a scene?"

Kristin brushed her off, "You didn't! Listen, apparently things usually get much worse at a Hawthorne gathering."

"Well that's good to know," May grumbled.

"I promise," Kristin replied, "Things went alright."

"And what about Ben?"

* * *

Kristin sighed, "Right. Ben. Well... I don't know if I should tell you this May."

"Trust me, I can handle it."

May didn't want to let Kristin know about her brief reconciliation with Ben quite yet.

"He ran out after you and his date saw… She was so angry that she made a confession in front of the whole room…"

"What did she confess?"

Kristin chuckled, "Well looking back I guess it's funny."

"Kristin, focus," May guided her, "What

happened?"

"She stood up in front of everybody cussing up a storm, saying that Ben had never even slept with her and that she'd slept with the manager of his restaurant in Las Vegas last month…"

"Jesus."

"Yep," Kristin replied, "It was pretty bad."

"So that's why no one remembered my outburst."

Kristin chuckled, "At least you're off the hook."

"Did you guys kick Ben out?" May replied.

Kristin sighed, "No. Zander tried to but I figured

we should let him stay."

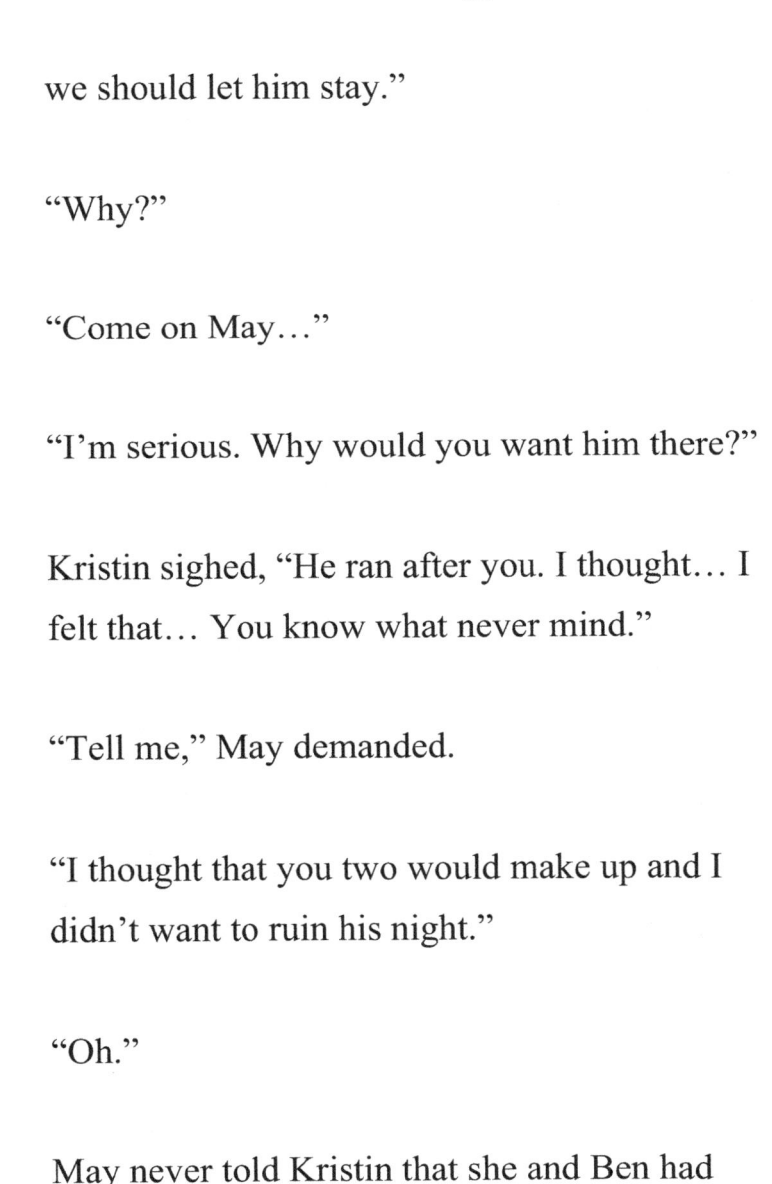

"Why?"

"Come on May…"

"I'm serious. Why would you want him there?"

Kristin sighed, "He ran after you. I thought… I felt that… You know what never mind."

"Tell me," May demanded.

"I thought that you two would make up and I didn't want to ruin his night."

"Oh."

May never told Kristin that she and Ben had

sort-of reconciled. And that she'd pushed him away all over again. For some reason, the subject was difficult to broach. May hung up the phone and let Kristin return to married life as she plunged into solitude once again.

This time, May was slower to recover from her break-up with Ben. As he'd promised, he didn't contact her and May couldn't bring herself to keep in touch with him. She had no clue what to say to him or how to talk to him without seeming like she was playing games. This wasn't a game to May. She either wanted to be with Ben or to be single. In-between couldn't work out anymore.

The problem with that was believing Ben was ready — truly believing it. May wasn't there yet.

* * *

It had been a month since she'd seen him. Ben had sent her a message for Mardi Gras — not a holiday that people usually celebrate. May hadn't bothered to reply. She'd been clear with Ben. She needed a reason to trust him before diving in completely again. She couldn't be lax with her heart anymore.

May was coming home from work on foot. As the weather grew warmer, she took the extra chance to get some exercise before her day began. May stopped at a café a few blocks from her house and took shelter from the cool weather inside. A hot chocolate would be the perfect cap to her day. She'd just finished walking her team through a big account merge and May was exhausted.

* * *

She stood in line, waiting patiently as the baristas called out orders and names. The warm, homey smell of the coffee shop took May's mind off work and when she ordered, the barista flashed her a friendly smile that reminded May there was more to life than the daily grind.

"Have a nice day now," She said as she handed over her $3.50 for the hot chocolate with extra whipped cream.

May waited on the side. A hand tapped her shoulder and May turned around sharply, expecting a familiar face behind her. Instead, she was greeted by a stranger. A beautiful stranger, but a stranger all the same.

The woman was darker than May with natural hair that was braided in two cornrows down the side of her head. She was tall — almost six feet — and had a wide smile with white teeth. Her nose was a gorgeous, wide nose and her lips were full.

"Hi," The woman said in a sweet, low voice, "I'm Megan."

"Hi…"

"You may not know me but you're May Roberts, right?"

"Yes… I am…"

"You're probably thinking that I'm some kind of crazy lady or something but I'm a friend of Ben's."

"Oh…"

"Congratulations on your engagement by the way."

"Huh?"

Megan looked down shyly, "Oh damn. I'm sorry… I thought that you and Ben were getting married…"

"Why did you think that?"

"I saw Ben the other night," Megan said, "Well, he saw me. He came over all flustered and said we could never see each other again."

Megan stopped and laughed, "Can you believe that guy? He ghosted me like eight months ago and now he's coming over talking about some woman he's in love with and how we can never see each other again. I figured y'all must be getting married."

"No. We aren't."

Megan chuckled, "Well you're lucky as hell because you seem to have cracked him. I never thought I'd see the day when Ben Hawthorne talked about settling down."

May nodded; she didn't know what to say.

"Well I'm sorry to disturb you ma'am but you're very lucky. Benji and I dated for a while and he was horrible to me. If he's cutting off all the women in his life, I assume he's found the one. I would be lying if I said I wasn't jealous."

May wasn't sure if she should apologize, or what she should say at all. Megan didn't seem to mind her silence.

"Listen, sorry for disturbing you again. I hope you make him very happy."

Megan collected her coffee and walked back out into the cold. May had considered walking home with her own cup of cocoa, but something compelled her to remain in the cafe and just think. Ben was up to something, but May had no clue what. She hadn't spoken to him, and for the first time since she had, May was beginning to think that Ben had changed.

One woman was hardly proof of all that, but May had seen the look of surprise in her eyes when she talked about Ben Hawthorne settling down. May had never believed that she (or any woman) could ever have the power to change a man but now that she was watching Ben, she began to wonder if she'd been wrong. Maybe if a man loves you enough, he'll provoke change on his own. Maybe it's not the woman that changes the man, but the act of loving a woman.

May had no clue. She was no expert on love. And even with Ben, she still had no idea what she was doing. May just wanted happiness. She wanted a clean, simple romance with action between the sheets. If Ben could give her that, then May would take him.

And still, despite that, May grappled with the word love. With Ben, she'd always feared that saying more would lead to receiving less from him. She worried that love would spook him. The thought of giving herself to Ben only to be abandoned terrified May more than just saying the words out loud. She hoped that Ben would be in a place to understand that.

When May finished her cup of cocoa, she continued her long walk home. When she arrived home, May hopped straight into the shower. She called her parents and she called Kristin. Kristin talked her ear off about Zander and how happy they were for close to an hour; May was just pleased that she didn't have to face another interrogation about her weird half-existent love life.

At 9 p.m. on the dot, Ben called May's phone.

She picked up fast. May wanted to act like she could ignore Ben but really she'd been waiting for him to call, desperate for him to show her something concrete since the last night they'd been together.

"May Roberts, can I come over to your place?"

This was different from the Ben she'd first met who'd barged in whenever he wanted to without a care in the world for May or her plans.

"Yes you can."

"I'll be there in twenty minutes."

With only twenty minutes to put herself together, May worked fast. She slipped into a pair of fitted black jeans and a white t-shirt. She threw her hair up into a ponytail and smeared a little bit of makeup on. May's heart was racing.

She hadn't seen Ben in a long time and every time they did see each other, a greater force than both of them always seemed to push them into each others' arms.

Tonight, May was ready for him. And when Ben showed up in exactly twenty minutes, she opened the door before he arrived.

"Goodnight Ben."

"Goodnight."

He jogged lightly until he was inside May's home. She took his jacket and hung it up.

"Come inside. Make yourself comfortable. Can I get you anything?"

* * *

Ben sat down in her living room, fidgeting with his hands.

"Uh… No…I mean…whiskey."

"Whiskey sounds nice but I won't be joining you tonight," May replied.

She poured Ben the straight whiskey and poured a glass of water for herself before she sat down. Ben poured half the glass of whiskey down his throat and then let out a gentle couch.

"'Scuse me."

"What's going on Ben?"

"You're looking for answers, right May?" He asked.

* * *

"Yes."

May was trying to hold it together but she couldn't hide her glee at finally seeing Ben again. Without strong impulse control, she could have hopped right into bed with him again. Logic be damned. Commitment be damned. It was hard to look into his gentle green eyes and not want more.

"I know I've been a pig. I know you want me to prove to you that I've changed. But fuck it May… I don't know how to prove it. I don't know how to do prove it without doing something crazy."

"I don't think you need to do anything crazy."

Ben shook his head, "No. No but I do. You think you know me May but you're not the only woman I've treated like shit."

"I guessed that."

Ben shot her an apologetic glance and then continued.

"I need to be honest with you May and I swear I'll get 'round to the point but I've just gotta be honest first."

"Then be honest Ben."

"This isn't easy."

May rested her hands on her lap. She knew this wasn't easy for him but she had a sense it would be even more difficult for her. She'd always had an idea about what kind of guy Ben was, but she'd never known for sure. Having definitive knowledge over how he'd really treated women over the years might change her mind about him. May had to take that risk. This was the only way they stood a chance, even if this hurt like hell.

"When we first started dating, I couldn't bear to be with another woman. I was hooked on you… like a drug. So I swear to you May from the first night we slept together I haven't looked at another woman the way I've looked at you."

His eyes locked onto hers earnestly. May waited in silence for him to continue. She wanted to hear every detail before she uttered a peep.

Ben sighed, "But it hasn't always been like that. I've been a dick... I've treated girls like shit who I didn't deserve and I did it because I could. I did it because they were easy. I did it because I had all the money in the world and I felt like that made me all powerful."

He paused and downed the rest of his whiskey.

"I broke so many hearts May and I just didn't give a damn. Hell, I'm lucky some of these women will even look me in the eye. When you told me I had to do better, the first thing I did was apologize. I apologized for everything that I'd done to 'em. I went through my shitty past and I faced up to it."

Ben was silent. Pensive. He let out a loud sigh.

"Just doing that made me realize that I. am. a. dick."

"Ben…"

"No don't interrupt me. I'm a dick. I don't deserve any of what I have because I've hurt people May. I've hurt you…"

"You've apologized."

"But apologies don't change what's already happened. And you're right. I need to change."

8 I Need Time

Silence hung in the air for a brief time as May looked towards Ben for him to continue. He seemed to be struggling to spit out his next words.

"This is hard for me."

"I know," May replied.

She really did understand. She had always understood Ben on a profound level which was a part of why after all he'd done she could stand to be around him. Ben was complicated. He'd always been complicated. But that was a part of why May loved him. Still, she was searching for the bravery to tell him.
That was up to Ben now.

"I've done something insane," Ben continued.

* * *

"What?"

Ben sighed, "I sold all my restaurants. *Hawthorne's* in town is the only one I have left."

"*All* your restaurants?"

Ben nodded, "Yeah. I haven't told you yet but my place in town isn't the only one that I own."

"Wait," May asked, "So you have more than one restaurant?"

"Yes. And I didn't tell you, I know that."

May thought back to Ben's ridiculously large house and the fact that he had a housekeeper. It made sense that *Hawthorne's* wasn't his only source of income. Still, it was a pretty big secret for him to keep.

"I don't understand why you kept that a secret."

Ben sighed, "I don't really get it either. You know, most times when I approach women it's what I start with. But I didn't want this to be about money between us May. I wanted it to feel real."

"Does it feel real to you now?"

Ben nodded, "It does. And… that brings me to my next point. I sold all my restaurants because I only want to focus on one thing — you. We can go anywhere in the world May. I'll do anything for you. We can go to Paris, Milan,

Bound & Gagged

Lagos… anywhere you want. Quit your job. Travel the world with me."

May felt her heart racing with the temptation to throw it all away and be with Ben. He'd rid himself of all his wealth just to be with her. He'd sold his life's work and he'd gotten rid of any female temptation from his past. He was here, looking at her with earnest green eyes and begging for a chance to prove to her that she was his one and only. And God, it was tempting to just close her eyes and take the leap.

May looked away from Ben and then pursed her lips.

"This is a lot to think about Ben."

He reached over and grabbed her hand.

Electricity sparked between them. May held onto his hand and looked into Ben's eyes.

"Don't think about it," He replied, "Just for one second can we stop thinking about things and just do what feels right."

"I don't know if I can."

"What more do you need from me May."

He was serious now; he had been since he'd entered her house.

"I promise you May, I will do anything that you need me to."

May nodded, "I know that Ben. I just need time to think. That's all."

* * *

"But you won't give me a yes or a no?"

May smiled.

"I know it's hard for you, but you'll have to wait."

"God woman… You drive me crazy."

May felt bashful. She knew that Ben wouldn't like it, but it was all that she needed — more time. May stood up and took Ben's hand, leading him to his feet.

"I need time Ben, but that doesn't mean you have to leave."

Ben looked into May's eyes and didn't find any

of the answers he was looking for. He saw how tentative she was to give him an emotional response, but he could also tell from the look on her face that she wanted him. He took a step closer to her; she didn't budge. Ben grabbed her waist and planted a kiss on her lips.

Thank God. It felt so much better to be kissing him than thinking about things. May had learned to be cautious with Ben and that was paying off. The second she'd raised the bar, he was striving to meet it. But still, it would be *insane* for her to give up her career on a whim. Love him or not, he'd have to wait. May began to undo the buttons on Ben's shirt. He shoved his tongue down her throat and gripped her ass cheeks more tightly as she reached for his chest. May trailed her finger tips down Ben's chest and pressed her hands against his rock hard abs.

With each breath, his muscles tensed. May could sense his cock rising in his pants as heat rose in her core.

May needed Ben's body now…

Answers would come later, but for now she needed a good hard climax to bring her to her senses and clear her mind so when Ben left she could figure out what to do next. Forever was a long time to commit to and she could tell that Ben wanted forever. Still, May had to be sure. And until her heart and mind aligned, she couldn't give him an answer that he wanted to hear.

"Fuck me…" She whispered.

The voice came from within her and begged for

her inner sexual goddess to be unleashed. May craved his touch. She craved the confidence in her body and in her sexuality that being with Ben gave her. She needed him to take her and use her body the way he'd used her the first night together. She needed pleasure that would make her shake and beg for mercy…

Ben lifted May off the ground and swept her off her feet with ease. It never got old how easily he could lift her weight. She was light as a feather in his arms and kept her legs wrapped around him as he carried her to her bedroom. Between kisses, they locked eyes with each other and made silent promises that this wouldn't — and couldn't — be their last night together.

Time apart didn't mean they were over this time. Ben threw May back onto the bed and stripped off his shirt completely.

"You're in for a wild ride sweetheart," He said with a grin.

"I can't wait for you to make me scream," May replied.

Sex with Ben always managed to be wildly invigorating and comfortable at the same time. He could bring her to an earth-shattering climax and awaken sexual desires she didn't even know she had.

Ben began to strip off his pants as May hurried to strip her clothes off. As she exposed every inch of her dark brown skin, Ben found his dick growing harder and harder. May's breasts were the perfect complexion with dark brown nipples the color of blackberries. Her smooth skin always responded so tenderly to his touch.

Ben slid into bed with May and started to kiss her all over. He planted kisses on her forehead and then moved his lips to her neck. May arched her head back, allowing Ben access to her sensitive flesh. He grazed his tongue along the flesh of her neck and then wrapped his lips around a piece of her neck tightly. May moaned as Ben sucked hard on her neck. Her pussy grew wetter as he kissed her.

May could feel pleasure exploding from that spot and she couldn't wait for Ben to thrust his hardness between her legs.

Ben's hands roved over her body and he squeezed May's bosom between his fingertips.

May whimpered as Ben pinched her hard nipples gently. He then moved his lips to her breasts and began to trace the outline of her areola with his tongue. May moaned and spread her legs wide as Ben's tongue pleasured her sensitive breasts.

Ben moved from one breast to the other until May was heaving with ultimate pleasure. He started to kiss her chest, then her tummy and moved his lips all the way down to her mound. May had a fleshy, hairless mound that led straight to her slick pussy. Before moving his tongue between her legs, Ben kissed her mound and spread kisses all over her thighs. May gasped as his tongue trailed across her thighs.

She grabbed onto a tuft of Ben's dark hair and began to guide his head closer to her wetness.

Ben smirked as he continued to tease her. He'd bring his tongue between her legs when he was good and ready. Ben teased May's thighs with even more kisses until he could sense she couldn't take it any longer.

He spread open her pussy lips and felt his cock jump as he stared at her wet pussy. May's honeysuckle scent began to fill up the room and her pussy lips were engorged with desire. May's clit sat between her folds a hardened nub, beckoning for him to taste her. May's heart raced as she felt Ben's lips closing in on her clit.

She loved him. She loved the way he knew how to take charge of her in the bedroom. She loved how many times she climaxed whenever they slept together. She was exposed to a never-ending slew of orgasms each time his tongue or his cock touched her wetness. And he was caring... so caring...

May moaned out loud as Ben's tongue massaged her clit. She grasped her bedsheets tightly and squeezed her eyes shut. The pleasure was incredible and nearly too much to bear. May cried out again as Ben began to stroke her clit with faster flicks of his tongue. He squeezed her thighs tightly and then started to push her legs back further behind her head.

With May's legs pushed back, Ben didn't just have access to her tight pussy, his tongue could slide all the way back to her ass. Ben began to lick May with long, slow strokes. She moaned loudly as she came closer to a big climax. Ben pressed her legs back and began to lick along the full length of her pussy, allowing his tongue to dip dangerously close to her asshole.

May groaned and exploded in climax. Ben's tongue massaged her pussy and then his tongue pressed against her asshole. When Ben's tongue touched her ass, May felt ecstasy unlike anything before. She gasped and then exploded again. As May writhed beneath him, Ben didn't stop tasting her. He let his tongue trail all the way back to her asshole as May exploded with climax after climax.

When Ben finally pulled his face away from her pussy, his face and her thighs were soaking wet. May was still trembling as she lowered her legs and gasped for breath. Ben wiped his face clean. His dick was rock hard and the veins traveling along the length of his shaft were bulging with his red-hot blood.

* * *

"I'm ready for you."

May was still gasping for breath. She sat up and looked at Ben, taking in the hunger in his eyes and the passion with which he'd just pleasured her. Hell, spending a life with Ben would never be boring, May was certain of that. But she couldn't make life decisions based off of orgasms alone.

Still, she needed him between her legs. She needed this physical confirmation of his love for her. She needed to see that Ben wasn't going to leave her again like he had in the past. She needed to be sure that his proof was genuine and that he was willing to wait.

"Then take me…" May replied.

* * *

Ben grinned, "That's my girl. Turn around on all fours…"

May obliged. She positioned herself on all fours, exposing her ass and pussy to Ben. She was still slick with juices from when he'd eaten her out. His cock jumped at the sight of her perfect pussy and her tight puckered asshole. Ben didn't just want to take her in one hole — he wanted both.

Ben began to massage May's ass cheeks and then he showered them with kisses. May wriggled her hips as she felt Ben's lips touching her curves. Ben rolled a condom onto his dick and positioned his hardness outside May's entrance. She was trembling from a mixture of euphoria and anticipation. Ben spread May's ass cheeks apart and began to slide his hardness into her pussy.

May whimpered and arched her back as the tip of Ben's dick slid past her entrance. May gripped the bedsheets as he began to push the rest of his dick into her pussy.

"Ohhh!" May cried out.

Ben gripped her hips and continued to thrust into her until his cock was buried deep in her pussy. Her tight heat gripped his cock like a vice. Ben grunted as he began to ram into her repeatedly. Damn. May was tighter and hotter than he remembered. Everything about her pussy was pure bliss. He grunted as he began to thrust into her wetness.

* * *

May groaned as Ben began to pound between her folds. The slipping between her pussy lips delivered jolts of pleasure to her core. May gripped the bed sheets and began to thrust her hips back to meet Ben's ardent thrusting. Ben pushed May's head into the bed and began to ram into her harder and harder.

"Oh yeah!! Oh yeah baby! Harder!" May cried out.

Ben squeezed her hips tightly and began to pummel her pussy. With each thrust, May got closer to a climax. She moaned as she felt her body heading towards a spectacular finish. Ben's thick cock seemed to be growing even more inside her and with each thrust, his dick came into contact with new parts of her pussy and delivered more and more ecstasy.

* * *

May gasped for breath as she thrust her hips back, knowing that a climax was going to come soon.

"Cum for me baby," Ben grunted, "Cum all over my big hard dick."

"OHHHH!" May cried out as she came.

She could never resist obeying one of Ben's commands. May writhed beneath him, sweating into her cotton sheets as she climaxed. She could feel the juices leaving her pussy and coating Ben's cock with her pleasure. Ben continued to pound into her as he felt her pussy spasming around his dick.

May stopped moaning as she gasped for breath.

The ferocity of her climax made her see stars and May found it harder and harder to breathe. For a moment, May could have sworn she blacked out. When she came to, Ben's dick was out of her pussy.

She gasped for a larger breath of air.

"Are you alright?" Ben asked.

May nodded, "Yes. I'm alright."

She was still panting and gasping desperately for breath.

"That. Was. Incredible."

She struggled with her words. Ben just smirked. It was about to get a lot wilder.

"Do you have lube?" He asked.

May nodded.

"I'm going to fuck you in the ass."

May looked back at him with concern.

"Don't worry. If it gets to be too much, you know what to do."

May nodded weakly and whimpered, "Mercy…"

"That's right. But I know you can handle it babe."

May wasn't sure she could. But she positioned

herself on all fours again. May flinched as she felt Ben squirt the cool lube over her asshole. He started slowly, massaging some of the gooey liquid into her puckered hole. Then he stroked the outside of her asshole, preparing her for entry.

At first, May felt squirmy and nervous. As Ben stroked her butthole, she started to get more comfortable. Ben slowly slipped his finger into her asshole and May was surprised to find that it didn't hurt a bit. It felt *good* — really good. She let out a soft moan as Ben began to plunge his finger deeper and deeper in her asshole.

Ben worked May's asshole until he was sure that she was nice and comfortable. He slipped a fresh condom onto his dick and positioned his hardness right outside her puckered asshole. Ben began to slide his dick into May's ass. She gasped as she started to grow accustomed to Ben's invading member.

He was so big that May expected his dick to hurt her. But she felt no pain, just a strange sort of pleasure that seemed to emanate from within. She gasped when Ben's full length was buried inside her asshole. Ben gripped her ass cheeks and began to pound her ass. May couldn't take it any more. She began to moan and writhe in pleasure. Ben grunted as he began to pound into her harder… and harder…

Pleasure began to explode in May's core. She climaxed in a way that she'd never climaxed before. She began to writhe and moan and again she started to see stars. As May gasped for breath, she started to cum…and cum.

* * *

Watching her experience a world of pleasure beneath him, Ben couldn't hold back himself. He let out a loud grunt as he came. His cock twitched while buried in May's ass and they both found themselves gasping desperately for breath.

After they'd made love, they lay in each other's arms all day.

She needs time to think... Ben thought to himself. And he planned to give her time. He had a good feeling that he knew what May would choose. After their morning together and after all he'd given up to be with her, he knew that she'd say yes. It made sense. *They* made sense. And no woman in her right mind would give up millions of dollars and traveling around the world — right?

When Ben left, he felt confident that he'd done the right thing. He'd worked his whole life for these restaurants and he'd given up on love. He used women because he thought he needed to give his business his all. And now, he had to choose love over business. May was worth making that choice for. Ben knew that in his heart.

9 Final Decision

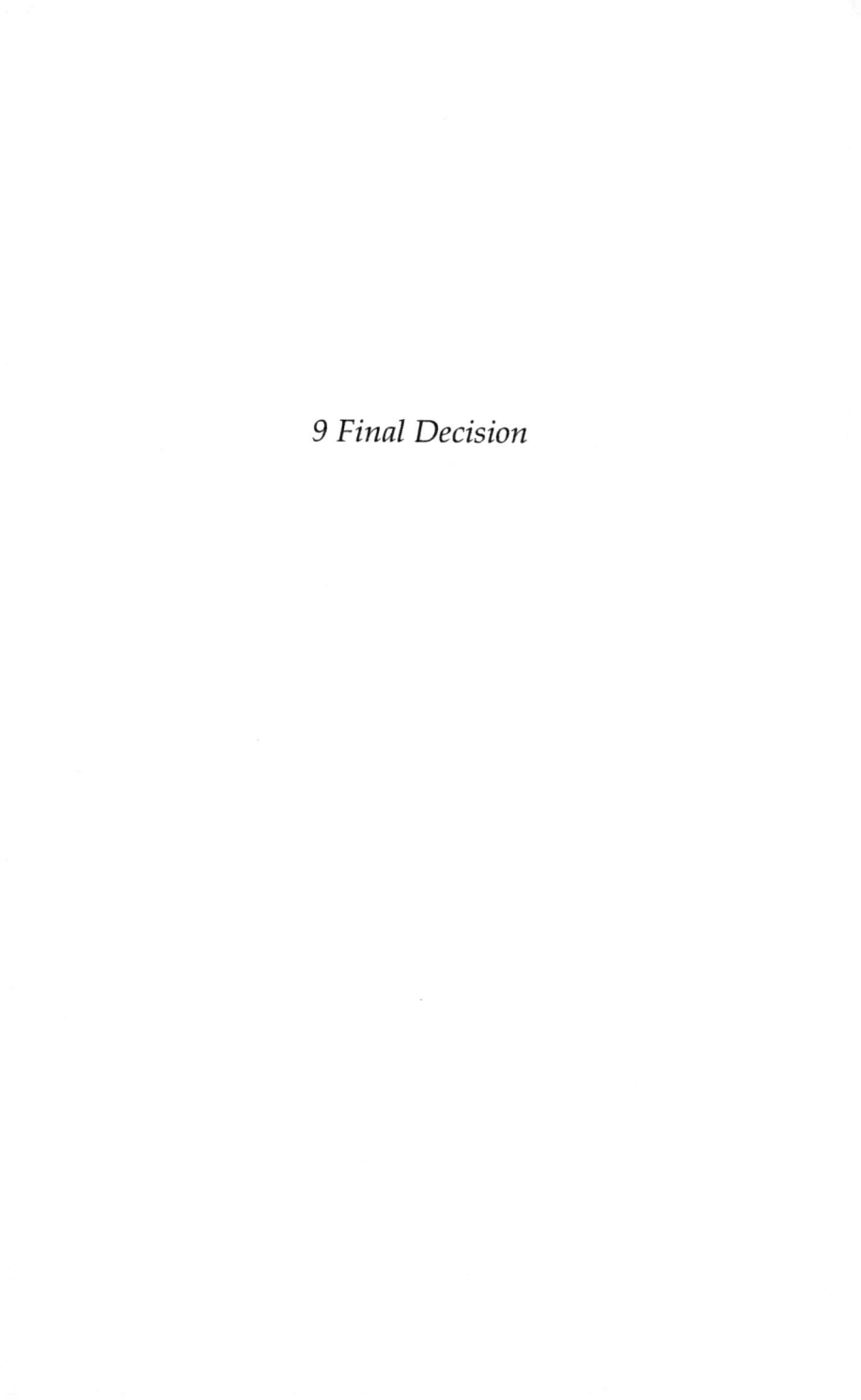

May stewed in her decision for weeks. She didn't know if she could turn to anyone for help — certainly not Kristin. After the explosion at Kristin's place, she doubted her best friend would be in support of a relationship with Ben. But he'd changed. May believed he really had. Still, was she making the right choice deciding to run off into the sunset with him? May went to work every day, reading a "good morning" text message from Ben before she arrived. Talking to him each morning brought her closer to him and the more May thought about him, the more her doubt melted away.

As much as Ben had hurt her, he'd also showed her a whole new world. With Ben, there was freedom that May hadn't experienced before. Before Ben, May had done what she thought was "right". She'd gone on bad dates with guys who she had no chemistry with. She'd stayed the beaten path in her career and risen to a comfortable (but boring) position. Ben promised excitement.

From the first time she'd stepped into his car, May had come alive. Ben had revived her passion for life. The more May reflected on this, the more she realized that the answer had been staring her in the face all along. Her fears about being with Ben were justified. But he'd changed. May had always found excuses why men weren't good enough. She'd always wished that she could find a man who was willing to change for her. And now that she'd finally found one, she was ready to shy away again.

After a couple weeks, May called Ben.

* * *

"Hey," He said.

May could hear how terrified he was. He didn't want to lose her. For once a guy was terrified to lose her. For once a guy was willing to give it all up to be with her.

"I want to see you. We need to talk."

"Jeez. That doesn't sound good."

"Can you just come over?"

"Yes. I'll be done crunching some numbers at the office around 6."

"So 7?"

"7's perfect."

There was a long moment of silence as neither of them wanted to hang up.

"Well I guess I should be going."

"Yeah. Right," Ben replied.

He hung up. May let out a long sigh. She couldn't wait to see Ben and put the confusing status between them behind her once and for all. She was about to do something big — something unlike anything she'd done before and May prayed that Ben would be worth the risk.

In the evening, May did everything as usual. She took a long shower after work and then she scheduled an appointment with her hairdresser for the next week. May made herself dinner and then got ready for Ben's arrival. He was on time, as usual. May watched as he approached her door, looking just as good as he always did.

He wore a sleek pair of black slacks a baby pink button down. His hair was slicked and combed back and in his hands he walked with a dozen red roses. May couldn't count them, but she knew Ben. That's the type of romantic he could be.

May opened the door and invited him. Ben handed her the flowers which instantly filled her home with a deep pungent fragrance. The scent of the flowers acted almost as a love spell.

May embraced Ben for the first time in weeks. Each time they reunited, she felt sparks explode between them. The gentlest touch could reignite the flames of her desires for him. Ben kissed her forehead. As his plump lips touched her forehead, May felt comfort — the comfort you feel knowing that you're about to make the right decision.

"Ben, let's talk."

"Please tell me you've got whiskey."

"White wine," May replied.

Ben nodded, "Well that'll have to do won't it."

May pulled the chilled Pinot Grigio out of her fridge and poured them both glasses. She took hers and drank a huge gulp. May knew she'd need the courage.

* * *

They stood there with both of their glasses. May was too focused on what she had to say to Ben to think about taking him into the other room.

"Talk to me May. I'm sick of waiting."

"I'm sick of waiting too. But this is hard for me Ben."

Ben's gaze remained rapt. He was sure he'd lose her. Ben's hand white-knuckled the glass which was luckily sturdy enough to withstand his firm grasp.

"I'm sorry Ben…" May started.

Ben felt his heart stop.

* * *

"I'm sorry that I've taken so long. I think I just needed to convince myself that you were real and that you wouldn't abandon me the moment things got real."

"What are you saying May?"

"You make me feel unlike any guy that I've ever met. You make me feel happy — euphoric really — but you piss me off like no other guy. It's not what I expected."

"And you're nothing like I expected."

May smiled, "But I have the answers Ben and I think… yes. I think we should be together."

Ben smiled and relaxed his grip on the glass.

"Yes? Yes to what."

"Yes. Let's travel. Let's see the world together. I want to be with you."

Ben shifted uncomfortably. He wanted to be with May but he didn't just crave her presence.

"This next part is hard," May muttered.

"What's hard?"

May sighed, "I love you Ben. Okay? I love you. And I know people will think I'm crazy for falling for a serial playboy. It seems stupid but it's how I feel."

"Don't feel stupid."

"Why not?"

"Because I'm different. Screw what everyone else believes. You know that I've changed."

May nodded, "I think I can believe that which is why this gets hard…"

"What's hard about this?" Ben replied.

He finished off his wine and rested it on the table.
"It's hard because I want to marry you Ben. I don't just want to be with you… I want to be with you forever…"

Ben was silent. He stared at May with his mouth slightly agape and his eyes boring into her. May wondered if she should have kept that aspect of her feelings for him private.

"Oh."

"Oh? That's it."

Ben chuckled, "Well, it's just that you sort of stole my thunder."

"Stole your thunder?"

Ben reached into his pocket for a black box. He set it on the table between them. May cast her eyes towards the box.

"What's in the box."

"Open it," Ben demanded.

* * *

May swallowed nervously and then opened the box. It was her turn for her mouth to hang open.

"Ben..." She whispered.

"Surprise," He replied with a grin.

"Ben, what is this?!"

"May... I know we've had our ups and downs. I know this whole thing may not make a whole lotta sense to people but from the moment I met you, I knew we had to be together. Forever."

"So this..."

Ben got down on one knee with the box in his hand. He took the ring out and grabbed May's hand. He could feel her hand trembling with anxiety as he slipped the ring onto her finger. Once the ring was on her ring finger, the shaking stopped. This confirmation of his love had given her the security she'd been looking for the whole time. This felt right to both of them.

"This means that I want you," Ben replied, "And I'll never stop wanting you May Roberts. So please, will you marry me?"

"Yes."

May nodded and tried to push back tears.

"Yes, Ben Hawthorne, I'll marry you."

Ben stood up and before May could say another

word he kissed her. Ben dipped her back and May felt a rush to her head as his lips pressed against hers furiously.

"I love you," She whispered as he pulled away from her.

Ben dove into kissing her again. This time their kisses were getting hotter and hotter. May knew how this would end. They couldn't get their hands on each other without it ending like this.

"Take everything off," Ben commanded.

May didn't need to hear him say it twice. She slipped out of her clothes until she was standing before him in just her underwear.

"Oh God woman… You make me so hard…"

Bound & Gagged

Ben grasped May's ass and pulled her closer to him as they made out. She could feel his hardness growing in his pants. May began to undo Ben's pants. The scent of the roses filled the air and seemed to get stronger as they began to kiss more and more passionately.

Ben lifted May onto the countertop and she wrapped her legs around him, pulling him close.

"Babe, I love you so much," Ben whispered, "Now take your panties off."

May slipped her panties off around her hips. Ben slipped his finger between her pussy lips, causing May to gasp for air.

"Oh yeah baby, bring that dick over here."

Ben slipped his pants and boxers off and positioned himself between May's legs. May could feel desire broiling between her thighs. Ben rolled a condom onto his dick and moved between May's legs. He began to slide into her slowly. As Ben began to gently push past her entrance, May let out a loud groan.

"Yes... Yes..." May whimpered as the first few inches of Ben's dick began to slide inside her.

He grunted and thrust in deeply, embedding his full length inside May's wetness. She cried out and grasped his back tightly. Ben began to plunge his dick between her legs. May cried out as she felt juices coating Ben's dick. His hardness was stretching her out and causing surges of pleasure to take control of her.

* * *

May dug her nails into Ben's back and moaned again as he began to thrust into her harder… and harder…

Ben began to work up a sweat as he plunged into May and she drew closer and closer to climax.

"Ohhh," She moaned, "I'm close… I'm close…"

"Cum for me baby…"

"YES! YES!" May cried out.

She threw her head back and allowed a climax to wash over her. Ben gripped her hips and continued to thrust furiously between her legs. As she moaned and trembled from climax, Ben lifted her off the counter still impaled on his dick and then laid May back on the couch.

The soft couch cushions allowed her to arch her back and expose her wetness to Ben. May threw her legs behind her head and allowed Ben to drive his dick into her deeper and faster. From this position, May found herself close to another climax yet again.

Ben pushed her legs back and began to pound into her pussy harder. May's pussy grew wetter and her thighs were coated in her juices as well as Ben's dick. He felt his cock stiffen as he came close to a spectacular climax.

He pressed May's legs back and groaned as he released inside her. When he came, he pulled out of her and they relaxed, naked on the couch as they caught their breath.

"Oh my God… that was amazing," May whispered.

She nuzzled up next to Ben. He kissed her forehead. It *had* been amazing but there was still room for more. He could still stand to taste May's flesh again and appreciate her.

"I think I'd like to stay the night," Ben asked.

May stuck out her hand, showing off the ring on her finger.

"I think you've more than earned it."

Ben grinned and kissed her again. May pulled away from him and closely examined her ring again. It was a single stone set on a solid gold band — exactly what she'd always wanted. May loved the simple and classic.

They finished around half the bottle of wine in celebration. Ben wanted to hop into the shower, so May followed him to her bathroom. While Ben was in the shower, she crawled into bed and picked up her phone to share the good news with Kristin. Confessing what was happening to Kristin was harder than when she'd finally confessed to Ben that she'd loved him.

May was surprised by Kristin's response. Kristin received the news far better than May expected her to. May wondered what had changed with her, but Kristin insisted it was nothing. Maybe her own marriage had just made her optimistic about love. May could have used the optimism. For the first time since she'd met Ben, she felt optimistic about the future and it was a wonderful place to be.

When Ben got out of the shower, May hung up the phone and ogled her fiancé's gorgeous body.

"Wow," She muttered.

"What is it?" Ben replied.

"You just look incredible."

"Yeah?"

Ben whipped off his white towel and stood before May fully naked. She bit down on her lower lip, unable to hold back. Ben's body was perfectly chiseled and the V shape on his hips traveled straight down to his dick.

"Get in bed," May pleaded with him.

Ben grinned, "Can't get enough of me, can you?"

"Unfortunately."

Ben climbed into bed with May and then began to kiss her again.

"This feels right, doesn't it?" He asked her.

May looked into her new fiancé's green eyes and agreed. Nothing felt more right than this. It had taken a while for her to get to this point, but now she saw what could be an incredible future together.

* * *

"Yes, it feels very right."

"Tomorrow, we'll work on all the details my love."

"Details?"

"Traveling the world. I was serious you know."

"I know."

May reached down between Ben's legs and grabbed onto his thick, ropey cock. She began to jerk his cock awake. As May grasped his cock, she could feel Ben getting harder… and harder…

"I want you again," May begged.

"Are you sure?"

May nodded.

"Then turn around on all fours…"

May turned around on all fours and exposed her wetness to Ben. He didn't hesitate this time. He thrust his dick inside of May in one swift motion. She gasped as she felt Ben's invading member.

"Yes…"

Ben gripped her ass cheeks and began to pound into her. As Ben drove his dick ardently into May's wetness, she felt herself approaching a quick climax. Her body was so responsive to

Ben that she knew it wouldn't be long.

"Harder..." She begged.

Ben gave her ass a nice big smack. May cried out and began to thrust her hips back as Ben obeyed her request and began to thrust into her harder... and harder...

He watched as May's thick ass cheeks jiggled against him and he eyed her puckered asshole which was tempting him to enter her from behind. Ben took his thumb and began to massage May's asshole as he pounded her pussy. His cock was again slick with her juices. The warmth of her body and the heat of her pussy was bringing him to another quick climax.

"Oh yes..." May whimpered.

* * *

Ben could tell she was close. He thrust his thumb into her asshole fully and began to plunge into both her ass and pussy.

May let out a loud moan as she climaxed. The euphoria she felt was indescribable. May gripped the bed sheets and thrust her ass back furiously as Ben pounded her. Pleasure overwhelmed her pussy and asshole as she came.

Ben couldn't take it. He spread May's ass cheeks apart and began to drive into her nice and slow. Ben groaned as he released a thick load of cum into May's ass cheeks. May moaned as she felt Ben's hardness twitching furiously inside her.

* * *

He pulled out of her and they lay side by side in bed for a while, coming down from the high of their individual climaxes. May stared at the ceiling for a few moments, wondering how she'd finally come to this point. She was in love. She was getting married. Soon, she'd be traveling the world with a man whose adventurous spirit had lit something inside of her that she'd never wanted to acknowledge existed.

Ben had brought something to her life that May hadn't expected. He was demanding, aggressive and dominant — everything she thought would repel her from a man. But underneath that was a protector, a strong man who would do everything in his power to keep his woman happy and safe.

***

That was what May had needed from a lover all along. That was what she had always wanted. And finally, she'd get her happily ever after.

Epilogue: May's Ending

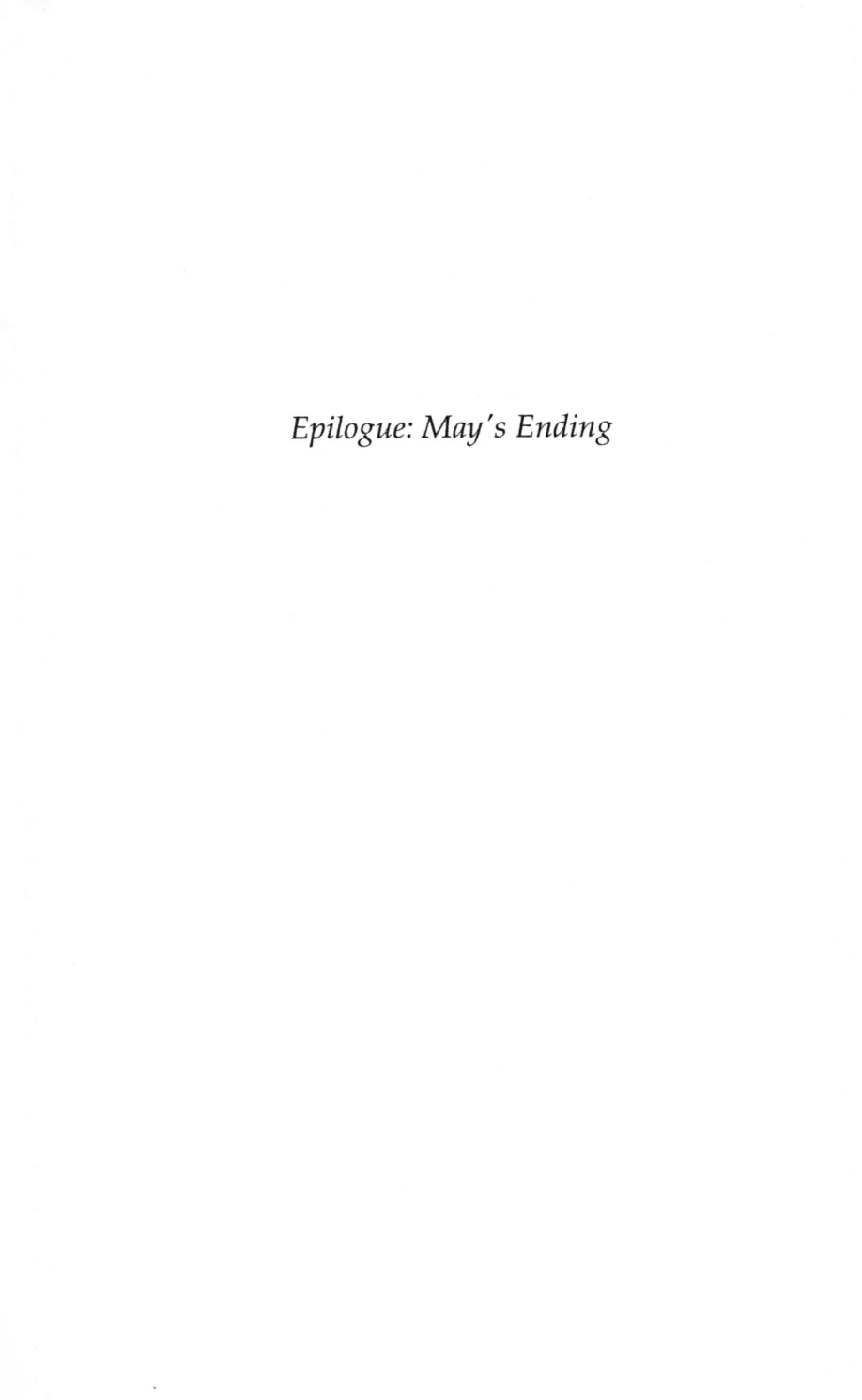

It was the start of another scene between the two of us. Sex had become more and more intense between me and Benjamin. I was starting to think that I would pass out from exhaustion after a particularly long scene and I wondered how I could maintain the erotic energy to appease him. As our bond grew deeper and more unbreakable, it became easy for me to slip into the role of his submissive — or whatever role he wanted me to slip into. I was *his.* In a way, he *owned* me. At least he owned my pussy. And I would let him do to me whatever he wanted.

I no longer worked; I dedicated my time to being Benjamin's housewife. He kept my account supplied with thousands of dollars each month. He hired a maid, a gardener and a chef so there wasn't really "housework" to speak of. And now, Benjamin was completely focused on seeding me with his son.

He was ritualistic, almost obsessive about the process of conception. I could tell it was a special thing for him. The scenes he concocted for us to act out required my complete dedication to him. My body and my mind became a part of his playground and nothing brought me greater joy than to experience the euphoria that I experienced when I surrendered to him completely.

Today, I was ready for him. I dressed up just as I was supposed to. Benjamin *loved* finding costumes for me to wear, outfits where I was dressed just by him and for him. I think it was his weird way of claiming ownership over me. And I didn't mind. The dress he bought me was a $500 black Kate Spade dress I'd been eyeing for Kristin's New Year's Party. Benjamin had also bought me two strings of pearls — I was wearing one string around my neck and another around my wrist. I adjusted my engagement ring and looked at the time. I expected Benjamin soon.

I heard a knock on my front door. In my six inch stilettos, I walked over to the door and tapped on it.

I walked towards the front door and opened it.

"Oh thank you! Thank you so much. I've been having so much trouble with my pipes… and well… my husband's away. There's really no one to help me fix things!"

Benjamin pushed past me and set his toolbox on

the ground. I have to admit his costume was convincing. He had on a worn blue jumpsuit with the first two buttons undone just enough that I could make out his grisly, strong chest. He had a tool belt strapped 'round his waist and a toolbox (which he'd just set on the floor).

He'd buzzed his hair and allowed his stubble to grow out quite a bit.

"Just show me where the leak is ma'am," He said.

I could barely tell it was him. I walked in front of him, taking my time to walk with ladylike steps. I knew he was checking out my ass, thinking of bending me over, thinking about pounding my pussy with his hardness.

* * *

I walked him to our guest bathroom and then threw open the door.

"There's a leak!" I said, gesturing towards the sink, which did indeed have a leak.

"Thanks ma'am," He muttered looking at me with discomfort and then darting his eyes away as if looking at me made him too nervous.

I walked away from the bathroom and returned to the kitchen. I heard him crashing around there and I knew what I should do next in order to keep myself nice and ready for him. I opened my purse and pulled my mini vibrator out of her case. I bent over the fresh, clean kitchen counters and hiked my skirt up to expose my pussy covered by a light strip of lace fabric.

* * *

Bound & Gagged

I took the small vibrator and turned it on, placing the tiny whirring machine against my clit. I stifled a moan as the vibrations sent instant jolts of pleasure shooting throughout my body. I slid the vibrator up and down the length of my pussy in smooth, slow motions, stroking myself to a heightened state of awareness.

Now, every sensation between my legs was heightened and I felt heat building there unlike anything I'd felt before. I felt so nasty with a plumber in my house and my pussy bared for all to see. I whimpered as I came. My legs trembled and I nearly lost my balance — I would have if it weren't for the counter top. My pussy throbbed and throbbed as ecstasy surged through my body.

I shuddered and tried to regain my balance.

Stars danced before my eyes and I moved the vibrator away from my sensitive clit. I looked forward to the next part of the scene but that didn't stop my heart's anxious flutter in my chest. With every scene, there was a certain element of uncertainty — especially with Benjamin.

I heard him stand up in the bathroom and I heard the door open. He was ready too. I slipped my vibrator back into my purse and stood up, smoothing my dress over my ass and pussy which were still hot with anticipation. A vibrator wasn't enough. I needed to feel this strong, sexy plumber bend me over and screw me against the counters of my own kitchen.

He walked into the kitchen and I looked at him innocently, "All done?"

* * *

"Yeah. All done," He said.

But he set his toolbox down again. He wasn't ready to leave.

"So er... Do you need a glass of water... What's your name again?" I asked.

"The name's Mikey," He said.

"Mikey, nice," I said flatly.

I had to feign disinterest. I had to get him riled up enough to want me badly. And trust me, I was ready to perform."

"And what's your name miss?"

"Oh it's *Mrs.,*" I corrected him, "I'm Mrs. May Hawthorne."

"Your husband must be some rich asshole huh?"

"I guess so."

I poured him a glass of water and walked across the kitchen to hand it to him. He looked me in the eyes just like he really was a strange. He betrayed no hint of who he really was. He had *become* Mikey the plumber.

"Does your husband satisfy you?" He asked.

"Excuse me?" I responded with surprise.

"You look like you could use a good pounding."

"Sir!" I replied, flustered, "That is *really* inappropriate."

"Do you like his cock?" He asked again.

This time, he flashed me a sociopathic grin and moved to position his body in front of the front door — my only exit.

I moved a step back and began to tremble my lower lip.

"I'm not the sort of woman to engage in conversation like this with strange men."

He grinned, "I know exactly what kinda woman you are. You're a bored, stuck up little housewife who needs raw, nasty sex. Your husband won't give it to you — or can't — so he keeps you in a cage. Well I'm a real man baby, and I'll give you whatever you want."

I looked at him with a blend of trepidation and desire.

"What if I let you," I asked meekly.

"What if?"

"Will you tell my husband?"

"It'll be between you and me princess."

I took another step closer to him. I could see his hardness already stiffening in his pants. He was hungry for my flesh. Would I remain so eager if I knew what he had in store for me?

* * *

"Please… Just don't tell my husband," I whimpered.

"Heh," He grunted, "I won't tell your husband but maybe he'll find out."

He pulled me into his arms and kissed me. I pulled away and pressed my hands against his chest.

"Mikey… Please be gentle with me…"

"Too late for requests princess, I'll take you how I want you."

He kissed me again and his hands fondled my ass and hips like he'd never touched a woman before. There was an animalistic hunger about him. He squeezed my ass cheeks and then reached up under my dress to grab them. His hands grabbed the string of my thong and he snapped it against my ass.

"Ow!" I whimpered.

He took his hands to my neck and grabbed my face, pulling it towards his.

"Don't make a sound unless I tell you to…" He growled.

I nodded; this time, the terror I felt was very real. He flipped me over and pressed my body against the counter. Benjamin would have kissed me more — but "Mikey" only wanted me for a quick and fast orgasm. I was his to use for the night. I was playing the unsatisfied housewife and boy was he gonna fix my pipes.

Bound & Gagged

* * *

Bent over in front of him, I was powerless. He hiked my skirt up and landed a full-palmed smack against my ass. Remembering his growling command not to make a sound, I only flinched in response to his hard touch.

I could hear him pulled aside his jumpsuit and I could feel the heat of his cock as he inched towards me.

"Please…" I begged, "Use a condom… If I get pregnant, I don't know how I'll be able to explain this to my husband!"

I could practically feel his smirking as he inched his cock closer to my wetness. I was sopping and I knew it would be an easy fit.

* * *

"I'll take you how I want to," He growled before shoving his entire hardness into my pussy.

I couldn't scream, he'd forbidden me from screaming. So the pain I felt instead reverberated through my body and caused me to tremble beneath his grasp. Feeling my hot, wet pussy clamping down on his hardness made him want to take me harder and faster.

"I'm going to cum inside you and put my baby in your belly… Now beg… Beg for it," He growled with a hint of sadism in his voice.

I wanted him so badly, that my begging sounded out like a pathetic whimper.

"Please… Please seed me with your big white cock…" I shuddered after I said the word 'cock'.

He gripped my waist tightly. I knew I was in for it. He began to pound into me hard and fast. I cried out, begging for him to plough me harder and begging him to cum inside my tight wet pussy. He grabbed me tightly and thrust into me deep and slow.

"Beg for my cum…" He grunted.

"Please… Cum inside me…"

I was close to a climax myself and begging him to seed me with his cum drove me over the edge. I let out a loud moan and trembled beneath his grasp again. He began sliding his dick into my tightness in a slow rhythm. I felt like I could cum again, but I also felt that he was close to finishing. I wanted him to finish. I wanted him to seed me and leave me bent over the counter top with cum dripping from my pussy.

"When your husband comes back you won't look at him the same. You'll always be thinking about Mikey..." He grunted and then began to pick up the pace as he thrust into me again.

"Yes! Yes! Take me Mikey! Cum inside my hot housewife pussy!" I cried out.

He began to thrust into me harder and harder. I clutched at the countertop but there was just enough slip for me to fail. All I could do was let him pound into me and wait for the explosion. It came soon. He groaned loudly and I felt his massive cock twitch inside of me over and over again as he coated my tightness with his seed.

* * *

He stood still for a moment, his cock twitched as he deposited more cum inside me. I gasped for breath. He raised his hands away from my body and began to pull away slowly. He pulled his cock out of me and tucked it back into his boxers. Then he tucked his body back into his jumpsuit.

"Ma'am. Don't move 'till I'm out of this house. I want you to remember who owns your pussy now… And it's me."

I nodded, too weak to do anything else. And I waited in the middle of my kitchen with my ass and pussy exposed. He picked up his toolbox and walked out. I felt his cum start to drip down my legs but I didn't dare move until he was gone. Disobeying Benjamin during a scene could mean hell to pay later. (He was still moody about disobedience.)

Once he was gone, I stood up and adjusted my thong and dress. My hair felt like it had been knocked out of place and I adjusted that too. I walked to our powder room and freshened my makeup. Just as I was done, I heard a voice coming from outside.

"Honey! I'm home," Benjamin called.

He'd only been gone fifteen minutes but the change was spectacular. The smell of his usual cologne permeated through the house as he entered the front door. His stubble was gone. He was dressed head to toe in his usual designer threads and his BMW was parked in the driveway.

* * *

"Hey honey," I greeted him and walked towards him with a smile on my face.

"Did the plumber fix the pipes downstairs?" He asked.

I nodded, "Yes he did. I think he did a good job."

"Excellent," Benjamin replied, followed by a wink. He opened his arms wide, gesturing that I come towards him for a hug.

I allowed him to wrap his arms around me and I pressed my nose into his neck, allowing myself to become taken by his sensual scent.

"Mmm," I mumbled.

* * *

He held me close and pressed his lips up to my ears, "You did very very well today May… I think you're owed a reward."

"A reward?" I asked.

"Yes…" Ben replied.

He pulled away from me and reached into his pocket, revealing a flat and long black box — big enough to hold a neck tie.

"What's this?"

"Open it."

I opened the box and gasped when I did.

* * *

The box was lined with velvet fabric and inside, there were two plane tickets to Havana and a glass butt plug with *Mrs. Hawthorne* engraved on it. It was kinky, but exactly what I'd come to expect from Ben.

"Do you love it?"

"Yes! Yes I love it!" I squealed.

"Perfect," He replied.

I covered the box and set it on the counter where I'd just been bent over.

"If you're good, maybe you'll get a taste of Mikey in Cuba," He said.

"I guess I'll have to be really really good," I

said, wrapping my arms 'round him again.

"Do you think you can handle it?"

"I think I can," I nodded.

"Perfect," Ben replied, kissing me again.

"I can't wait to marry you," He added.

I couldn't wait to marry him either — I'd done enough to earn the title of Mrs. Hawthorne.

Made in the USA
Middletown, DE
10 October 2024